About the Author

The author is a native of the island of Trinidad and Tobago. She is curious about life, loves to swim in the warm Caribbean Sea and to go on hiking adventures. She listens to a wide selection of music and loves a good story regardless of the genre.

The Neutral Zone
Citizen of Androfemur

J. I. Gonzales

The Neutral Zone
Citizen of Androfemur

Olympia Publishers
London

www.olympiapublishers.com
OLYMPIA PAPERBACK EDITION

A CIP catalogue record for this title is
available from the British Library.

ISBN: 978-1-78830-614-0

This is a work of fiction.
Names, characters, places and incidents originate from the writer's
imagination. Any resemblance to actual persons, living or dead, is
purely coincidental.

First Published in 2020

Olympia Publishers
Tallis House
2 Tallis Street
London
EC4Y 0AB

Printed in Great Britain

Dedication

I dedicate this novel to my mother, who lives with glaucoma and is unable to read for herself. I would never be able to read this book to her on account of its raunchiness, however she allowed me to geek out on books as a child and thus she is the reason why I am addicted to writing.

Acknowledgements

I want to acknowledge Lisa Clarke, Shakeema La Foucade and Junia Ali, my friends who encouraged me to keep on writing this particular novel. I also wish to acknowledge a man who has been more than a father, and a great friend to me, Phillip A. Wilson, attorney-at-law.

CHAPTER 1

Jane:

Marriage! What a thought. I placed the history book at the left side of my bedhead. I was careful enough to buy this old book in an antique store by bartering an ornate German Cuckoo clock which was left to me in Aunt Elise's will. I couldn't chance researching the topic online, never knew what spy software was on my laptop or desktop. The Separatist police kept a keen eye on their investments.

My thoughts strayed back to the topic at hand. Marriage? What were people thinking of to have carried it on for so long? A well-documented record of marriages on every continent spanning back as far as four thousand, four hundred and twenty-nine years? Well it had finally come to an end in our part of the world, legally of course. Twenty years ago, people still did midnight ceremonies hiding from the Acquittal Marriage Enforcers (A.M.E), but even that had ended since The Separation.

Good idea in theory, The Separation. Painful in reality of course. Wasn't everything in life like that? So it seemed anyway. It's like how women always obsessed about bouncing babies, but childbirth was such a mess. I had seen it once or twice, so excruciatingly painful. However, in the end mother and child always seemed to be happy, all smiles, pain forgotten. Life was like that in a way, every good thing was born out of pain. The Separation, an idea, a cause and now law was what I lived for. It was the answer to end all disease transmission and save the race called mankind. It was the natural conclusion to the abolition of marriage as a rite of passage.

Nevertheless, all I could think of was the look in that woman's eyes when she was handed over by the Maleside border patrol officer. She knew if she wanted to enter the Neutral Zone, she had to apply for a work permit. But she didn't want to work in the Neutral Zone did she? She wanted to cross to the other side, to Maledrome. Forbidden, unheard of. To find an old husband, she said. Had she not been so old, so fragile, I would have dealt her two back hand slaps as she kept on babbling about "love". I myself thought she was talking about a dove all that babbling, all that saliva. So unnecessary.

I had seen women fall apart when they handed over their male offspring at the end of the weaning period. I could understand becoming attached to your own flesh and blood. The wee things, so helpless, given over to where they belonged — Maledrome.

Who wouldn't be afraid to handover their offspring to that place where it seems that even God had forsaken? There were stories of Maledrome, wild, dreadful, hair raising stories. Most of it was fiction and told to us ladies so we would never get it in our heads to cross over into the Neutral Zone. Men and wars, men and animals, men and men, men as beast. Ghastly stuff to scare little girls and of course, the dreaded, disease festering Neutral Zone.

I was trained in combat skills for my job but we, the citizens of Androfemur, had never known about wars or diseases. Skirmishes, disagreements, disputes, but never wars and diseases. Wars and diseases were associated with men, and we the women of Androfemur, had never known men. Unlike the other women of my generation, I was fortunate enough to glimpse the border patrol men through the one-mile walk-way fence, but they only appeared as specs from my limited view. The thirty feet tall barb-wire fence between our two territories acted as a constant reminder that we were prisoners of our own existence and the Charter between our two zones only theoretically held an agreement of rights and freedoms.

Women were impregnated via artificial insemination. We kept to our side and handed over the male offspring after the weaning period. The men kept to their side. We, the Adrofemian, never knew the touch of a man's rough, gritty paws. Men's semen was scrutinized in the National Scientific Lab for Diseases Annihilation, where imperfections were contained and destroyed. The only males we encountered at Androfemur were babies. When seen in public they were always a spectacle, not because they looked different from any other baby but because mothers required blue ribbon permits which were to be displayed by law to transmit a man-child from one dwelling to another. Other citizens, by law, were encouraged to stay away from their carriages. I guess male babies were kind of like our modern-day lepers.

My mind descended from a wandering cloud as I returned to reality. I was to report for duty in an hour but I still sat up in bed thinking through a veil, while replaying the old woman's desperate pleas for assistance in finding her husband. What was I doing, getting caught up in this nonsensical business? Yet it was so strange, surreal even, that she would be so insistent after twenty-three years about an old husband, but that she was. The tear streaked face: the torn blue shirt, exposing where she used bandages to conceal her female form. She had disguised herself as a man to defect to the other side. Determination motivated by her desire to be in the arms of her husband again was all I could see in her eyes as she fought, her fingers and forearms bled, clawing their way away towards an imaginary husband. Dressed in a navy blue shirt and khaki wranglers, with her salt and pepper hair tucked under a baseball cap, she apparently tried to make her get up look as effortless as possible. Some people were really weird.

I censured myself. What was really bizarre was the fact that I was still thinking of this foolishness, wasting my time when I should be leaving my house to get to work.

It would be my first time in the Neutral Zone tonight. I was to supervise in the conveying of ten female prisoners to the Neutral Zone. All of Androfemur's female prisoners were sent over to the Neutral Zone as punishment, to contemplate the error of their ways, but I found out that some people intentionally got arrested or applied for work permits to go to the Neutral Zone. On purpose! Weirdos.

It would be my first assignment to the Neutral Zone. I admit I was a bit curious, but it was also a big night for me because a promotion might be involved. OK, OK, I must admit I was a bit more than interested about all the stories, you know men coexisting, cohabiting with women, especially after yesterday's incident. Added as a bonus, I was to see a man up close and in person tonight. I had never seen a man before, not up close anyway and I was to personally hand these women over to the custodian in charge of the Neutral Zone. I was told that the custodian was a he, not a she. I thought it strange that they would send a man to do a woman's job but I was told that the arrival of the new girls was always a spectacle, and that the men got a bit carried away, so they needed one of their own to deal with the situation. Men — such animals! Fine by me as long as I didn't have to deal with too many of them at once. One was just enough for me to scrutinize and form my own opinion.

As I got into the shower the water, which always ran a bit too cold, stung my skin but the sensation went unregistered as my focus was pulled recalling yesterday's briefing. I was briefed by the Chief Superintendent who reminded me that men were not to be dealt with like how we dealt with each other.

She barked, "They are all liars, so don't bother looking him in the eyes when you hand over the girls and the papers. And, oh," she said as a last thought, "don't even bother shaking his hand either. Don't know where they've been. A nice pair of gloves should do the trick."

She continued, "After which you are to receive five women at The Midwalk point, kill two birds with one stone. Wait in the accommodation set up for you until they have all arrived at the drop off point. Those are your orders."

And just like that I was dismissed. It was a bit overwhelming being in the presence of Superintendent Claudia. She was a large, no joking, matter-of-fact old-school puritan, but she was well liked and always fair. Her orders were always followed to the last dot of every 'i'.

I had been with The Separatists Police for nine years — four years at the rank of sergeant. I had impeccable timing, and a willingness to do what it took to get the job done. Some called it courage, others called it just plain crazy. Nevertheless,

I was rewarded with two promotions before the age of twenty-six because of my exploits. It was no secret that it was my ambitions to enter the first division rank before thirty and so this assignment was of great importance to me, career wise.

It was time for me to leave the house to get to work. The beautiful brand-new BMW Electronext series parked outside of my house was a perk of the job. There were only 500 motored vehicles which included cars, trucks, tractors, and boats operational in the territory, everyone else got to their destinations via bicycle, or Ambient Air rail in an effort to keep carbon emissions low. She was black, sleek, graceful, so unlike the owner — tall, skinny, lanky, but hey, if you were lucky you could pick the car you drove, what you couldn't do was pick your genes, not until after you were born anyway. And as tempted as I was Prime Editing was not for me, I couldn't afford it on a state salary besides I got too accustom to this face staring back at me in the mirror. In any event, I was not all skin and bone. My exterior hid steely corded muscles, which I was very proud of. More importantly, I worked extremely hard to upkeep my physic. Turning thirty this June was not a prospect that I relished. It wasn't difficult to figure out why it got so much harder to run a mile in five minutes at my annual physical evaluations. But hey, growing old was not too bad, at least I would have an extra minute and a half to complete the annual mile run after hitting the big three O. Not that I was planning on needing it. I still held the department record for the fastest time, four minutes and five seconds.

As I drove past the street before Headquarters, I could hear the community leader announcing yet another meeting concerning neighborhood issues. This neighborhood in particular was notorious for putting their waste in the wrong bin. I mean, why was putting green bottles in the green bin, white bottles in the translucent bins, plastics in the opaque bins, tins/aluminums in the grey bins, vegetable/fruit waste in the yellow bins and other materials in the brown bins such a hard concept? These citizens really needed to get it together before the Environmental police intervened in the matter.

As I drove passed the guardroom sentry I took a glimpse at my dashboard for the time. The solid stare of blue neon lights displaying 5:15 p.m. looking right back at me. I was on time, no surprise there, the new law encouraged citizens to stay off the road between the hours of five p.m. and seven p.m. to aid night time shift workers, especially service personal, to get to work on time. Residents of the Agrarian Sector argued that the majority of the traffic was non-motor vehicular and that their workers just wanted to get home after working in the fields all day. Despite the Agrarian sector's misgivings during the special vote which passed this bill, the 'Ease Traffic' legislation was really working out well.

I guess for some the Utopia was more elusive than for others. There were some especially those from the Agrarian sector, who believed it to be more prison than paradise. There were words and phrases which were held to cause division between women. Words like black people, white people, yellow and red people, Negro, European, Asian that were retired from use in official language and text, but historical baggage was more tenacious than an ideal and messages were conveyed in more than just words. The fact that the people of the Agrarian section looked more like me was no coincidence.

I was one of the lucky ones because my mother died during childbirth which meant I wasn't automatically relegated to born, live and die in the Agrarian sector. As a ward of the state I went to live with an 'Aunty' who lived in the

Vreeland sector. I guess some animals were still created more equal than others.

I approached my pigeon hole, confirmed my identity and jumped my orders from the mainframe unto my Pilot Infinity. As I scrolled down I realized they were very straight forward, requiring me to carry out certain functions at particular times.

Tonight

7:00 pm Roll call for prisoners (check profiles with actual faces)

7:20pm Walk to the transport

7:30pm Load prisoners onto transport

7:50pm Transport leaves docks

9:00pm Arrive at Androfemur Outpost and report arrival to Watch Commander

10:00pm Hand over prisoners to custodian

10:00pm Collect receipt slips for prisoners

10:20pm Resign to quarters on base.

Next day

Wait for call concerning released prisoners

Collect released prisoners at Midwalk point

Roll call for prisoners

Catch transport arranged by Watch Commander

Load Prisoners

Return to Androfemur

This was going to be a piece of cake.

CHAPTER 2

There were two entrances to Maledrome — the Maledrome border patrol entrance which was accessed via the Midpoint Walkway and the Androfemian Outpost. Both were pretty secure as all citizens needed papers to cross either way especially into the Neutral Zone.

As people would, over the years they found other ways to enter and exit besides these two legal checkpoints, but those were secret even to people like Superintendent Claudia. This was why they were still in existence. A very select few really knew where they were located. Hopefully very soon part of my job would be to locate these breaches and close them. Just as soon as I got my promotion, having already sat the entrance exam, I would be eligible to apply to the section called the EBPB. Only highly decorated officers at and above the rank of inspector were permitted to join the Elite Border Patrol Bureau and that is just where I was headed, if I had my way of course. I had to agree that accepting this assignment was a step in the right direction.

While standing in the locker room, I hooked the last silver button of my uniform into place. My mind drifted back to the inhabitants of Maledrome and the Neutral Zone and all the myths surrounding these two territories as I absentmindedly pulled down the peak of my forage cap settling it deeper onto my head.

Contrary to popular belief, the Neutral Zone was not independent of the two territories, Androfemur and Maledrome. One only had to take a look at the territorial map to realize that the Neutral Zone appeared as a territory in Maledrome itself, about ten miles from the entrance of the Maledrome border patrol station. Technically speaking, all Androfemians considered the Neutral Zone to be part of Maldrome and just as corrupt. However, we were always led to believe the Neutral Zone was festering with the worst types, waste collected in the cracks of the most humid place of Hades and if there was a hell, the Neutral Zone was its entrance. At least, that is what my Aunt Elise always said. Tonight I would see some of it and make my own judgments. I could feel my excitement building as I surveyed my ten prisoners. Small time offenders, mainly littering, loitering offences, petty theft, nothing major. However, all prisoners were required by law to be cuffed and chained during transportation. I retrieved the data cache that was prepared for me with their names, pictures, descriptions, psychological profiles, crimes, sentencing and release dates. I stuck the drive into my Pilot infinity, scanned the prisoners' implants and compared their individual profiles; confirming each individual identity. All ten turned out to be a match. No surprise there, the Separatist police of Androfemur rarely ever made mistakes.

"Come on, let's go. Shuffle forward, move," I shouted to the prison gang. No one spoke. They all moved forward, trying to get the timing of the other so they wouldn't be yanked forward or fall headlong into a pile-up whilst still being dragged on account of the chains attached to their feet and hands.

We got to the bus in no time and I unattached every single hand and foot cuff and secured it onto the horizontal bus poles designed to hold prisoners for transport. Before I could say *Sam was a sparrow*, we were off, these women to their sentencing and me to satisfy my curiosity of the Neutral Zone.

I felt, as I sat to the back of the bus, like I was six again and on my first field trip to the zoo or somewhere I had been longing to visit. My job shouldn't be this fun, I thought, but no one would guess my thoughts as I kept a stern face for my charges in case they tried to escape. Not that in the record of transporting prisoners anyone was ever successful in the few attempts that I knew of. I was tempted to ask the offenders prone to recidivism their opinion of the Neutral Zone but I didn't want to get too familiar with them. It was a shame, though. I felt like I was going into my adventure like a Cyclops with a glaucomic eye but then I guess it wouldn't be an adventure if there was no mystery.

Although I was advised to retire to my quarters I had no intention of doing so tonight, not straight away anyway. I had it all planned. I would go out and walk the streets a bit, maybe go into a bar or two — disguised of course — and that would be it. One hour, two, tops. I had to get my own impression of the territory. No more gossip and guessing for me, I would see the Neutral Zone first hand. Tonight.

Katie Hammond and I met on a Human Trafficking seminar five years ago and we remained friends ever since. She was stationed at the Androfemian Outpost and during one of our infrequent lunch dates she promised to loan me her car to have a night out on the town whenever I made it around to the Outpost. She assured me that it was not as bad as the rumors had it but that even the female officers at the Outpost loosely observed a curfew. No one really stayed out passed two a.m. I had no intention of staying out after twelve-thirty a.m. I had been studying Ingo maps ever since I got the idea to visit the Neutral Zone, however my plan was simple. I intended to follow the transportation that was taking the prisoners away, if the transport went into a town or any other populated place I would stop, and have a look, if it seemed safe. If their destination was to a rural area, I would stop observe the scenery from the car and use the car's GPS system to return to base. Maybe I would do something more adventurous if and when Katie had a night off. Unfortunately, she was on duty tonight.

The Outpost was a well-kept, two-storied, red brick building enclosed in a circular twelve kilometer perimeter of electrical fencing. It looked a bit lonely as we drove up. There were four cars parked near the station building and a big yellow bus which was idling at the entrance of the Outpost. I knew it was running because I could see the tailpipe sending streams of black smoke into the atmosphere. That was something I had never seen in Androfemur however, I knew about these vintage buses that had been taken off the street by our Environmental police about eighteen years ago.

In my youth I'd fantasized about becoming a mechanic, my curiosity born out of a passion for vehicles of all types. Once, on a visit to the Gremmel National Museum, I recalled being so intrigued by the idea that years ago vehicles ran on fuel, cars mainly on petrol and trucks on diesel. I kept asking myself, wasn't it obvious that extracting a substance from the earth was contributing to global warming? What I really couldn't understand was that electric vehicle technology was invented before the turn of the twenty-first century. The effects of global warming were well on the way, the polar bears and other arctic species became extinct and yet world leaders could not get their heads out of their asses long enough to institute a global ban on drilling for fuel.

Truth be told, world leaders never really got their shit together until a movement of graduate mothers began to invest in electric cars and sustainable energy. Some said it began as a cult and it was a movement doomed to fail, but all Androfemian's knew the words of Shelly Maz, a co-founder of the movement. "If a single tree falls then one can deny it existed but if all the trees were to fall no one in their sphere could deny the deafening sound."

The granting of the Northeast Greenland National Park to Shelly Maz and all those women who first joined her was the dawn of a new era of women making decisions by themselves and for themselves and would change the course of history forever.

We were taught at school that all the political pundits expected Maz and the others to fail. The landscape was unchartered, it was vast and untamable. They gave the "little ladies" a couple months in the cold so that they would all shut up and run back with their tales between their legs. I occasionally wondered if the politicians would have ever humored the movement had the polar ice caps not melted and the sea levels not risen by nine feet, causing the extinction of ninety percent of all Artic life. Whatever the motive Maz and the other Matriarchs renamed the territory and never looked back.

Outside the bus there was a person — male or female I couldn't tell — standing extremely still with a grey hooded jacket and hands stuck in his/her pockets. It was such a strange scene because it could have been about five degrees below zero outside. Who would want to stand out in the cold when they could wait in a warm bus? I instructed the driver to pull up next to the entrance of the Outpost. As I was about to alight the transport to report our arrival and enlist some help in offloading my cargo, the weight of the bus shifted. I looked up into a pair of chocolate brown eyes with dark sooty lashes. A nose which may have once been beautiful but had obviously been broken more than once. My eyes rested on a pair of full lips, his entire face a contradiction of soft features that endured a hard life. The rest of the face was hidden by a hoodie.

I took in his stature; so this was a man. This specimen exuded an animalistic virility that was palpable. Corded muscles bunched beneath his sweater, his 6 feet 4 inches may have intimidated a lesser mortal. I took a whiff of him, naturally anticipating the stench I was informed was associated with men but instead I was surprised by the subtle but sensual fragrance of juniper berries and something else I couldn't place my fingers on.

"I'll take over from here if you don't mind," a very deep voice emanated from beneath the hood.

I stood staring in surprise at the rudeness of my unknown uninvited passenger. "Excuse me?" I caught my tongue in time.

"Look, love, here is not the only place I have to be tonight. You've wasted enough of my time," his response cavalier but yet managing to demonstrate his impatient at the same time.

24

This guy's impertinence was monumental. I kept on opening my mouth and closing it, until I enquired, "Who are you?"

Hoodie guy slipped off his hood, revealing a full head of flaxen blonde hair, fished into his pockets and produced a slip without saying another word. His left eye brow shot up as if he was annoyed that he had to identify himself.

"OK, nice to meet you, I guess you are my guy… I mean the person I hand over to," I said, attempting to bring civility to the matter.

"Hey, I would love to stand and chat or even buy you a drink later, but neither of us are getting any younger," he said as he tried to slip past me.

I sighed. He was an asshole, but what was I expecting, Sir Galahad? I stuck my forearm out and blocked his path. "I am sorry but there are some procedures that I need to follow. If you care to follow me inside."

He stopped in his tracks, rocked back a bit, peered intently in my direction and changed his stance. From my perspective it appeared that he came to the conclusion that he made a monumental error by attempting to rush me so he switched tactics by changing the tone of his voice which was accompanied by a sweet sympathetic simper. "I get it you're new, but here's the thing. There is really no need for all this pomp and ceremony, I usually take the girls straight off the bus and I'm on my way," he interjected, smiling, revealing two really alarming dimples right below his cheek bones but I was not having my first assignment screwed up by some eager guy even if he had an interesting face.

"Now you are wasting my time. I recommend that you step away from my path, so that you can let me do what I need to do, is that OK?" I asked in my sweetest tone.

I could tell he was seething with anger but he stepped out of my way, allowing me to go to the Outpost, report my arrival, collect Katie's car keys and quickly change. I returned to the bus to offload the prisoners. When they were safely on Hoodie's transport, he signed my Pilot Infinity and he was on his way, pulling away from the Outpost with relative fury as soon as I disembarked.

How discourteous! My feet had scarcely left the bus when he pulled off and I was planning to follow him off the compound. Belatedly realising the bus was getting away, I raced to Katie's car and pulled off with a cloud of dust behind me in pursuit of the bus which was now a speck in the distant night. Wow he was really aggressive with the accelerator pedal, I thought as I tried to play catch up. I chided myself for my ingratitude as I thought that my BMW would have narrowed the distance in no time at all.

How uncouth, he could buy me a drink indeed! Did I look thirsty to him? Stupid guy! Were all the species so indecorous?

And what a jerk. He wanted me to rush through the procedure so he could be somewhere else. I was on time and not a minute later. He should not have double booked, then he wouldn't have been worrying about some other meeting at another location.

Imbecile, idiot!

I finally caught up to the bus and soon we were at an intersection, me sitting in fumes coming from the bus's tailpipe. I looked up and saw street lights, swishing wipers on cars, tall buildings constructed too close together, electrical wires overhead, men and women walking the street, walking really fast. I rolled down my window to get a closer feel of the place. The thickness of the smog choked me as I inhaled the night air. It was thick, polluted and I resisted the urge to claw at my throat.

As the bus pulled off, turning right, out of nowhere someone walked up to the front of my car. I also felt another presence standing behind the window of the driver's side door. My instincts kicked in and I pulled off, swerving to the side of the person standing in front of me. That was close. My police training just avoided me being mugged or probably worse. I looked at the car clock. The time on it was 10:20 p.m. I would drive around for another half hour and then I would return to base.

By now the traffic was so heavy, I had lost sight of the bus. I had no intention of coming out to go anywhere, not after my near mugging incident, when I saw the Yellow bus, same registration number parked outside a three-storey building.

So this is where Hoody had to rush off to be? Dinner? Probably meeting a woman as well. I still could not imagine men and women actually coexisting in my time but hey this was the Neutral Zone. All sorts happened here.

The building really drew my focus. It was a fairly respectable establishment even by my standards, aged stonework, twentieth century, really classy. I pulled up in front of the building, wondering why I was stopping, when a young woman dressed in what seemed to be some sort of uniform walked up to my window and said, "Good night, ma'am, this way please." She indicated the direction with her palms stretched out, pointing to the entrance of the building.

She could only be the valet and this must have been a restaurant. At that point in time my stomach chose to remind me that I had not eaten since lunchtime. I was hungry enough to eat a bear. I thought about it for exactly two seconds then climbed out, convincing myself that there was no way that I could give a credible report of the Neutral Zone if I had not at least left the car to take a closer look. I decided this is where I would dine tonight. As I was taking a closer look at the brass name plate at the side of the door *The Wrestler's Restaurant and Club*, the heavy double doors opened for me and I stepped into the foyer.

The interior left the exterior wanting; I could smell the scent of exclusivity in the leather upholstery in the foyer. On display were twenty-first century Chinese bamboo shoot arrangements emerging from a white stoned inside water fountain, beautiful 1960s wall art décor of female models scantily clothed, dark marble floors and tastefully done oils created by an unknown artist. The lighting was low, which gave the setting an intimate feel. Looking up I observed a big, well-dressed man descending the winding staircase. He had an item in his hand, something like a napkin, with which he was doing his best to wipe his hands as he descended quite gracefully.

As he approached in my direction, I made my observations he was well balanced, no doubt trained in ballet or martial arts. The flinty look in his eyes, combined with his composed features, encouraged me to think the latter.

"How wonderful of you to grace us with your presence, sergeant. We were just about to have dinner. Would you care to join us?"

The invitation, although politely extended, sounded more like a threat if I had ever heard one. I reasoned that I could run, but this man already seemed to know more about me than I knew about him. Therefore I accepted the offer by taking the extended hand.

As I ascended the meandering stairwell, I wondered at his choice of words. How wonderful of you to grace "us", not "me", with your presence. Obviously, there was a third party involved and we were on our way to meet him.

A quick tally, allowed me to count — I had only met five people in the Neutral Zone. First was Katie, who I knew. The second, third and fourth — I only met tonight — the night duty staff at the Outpost, Constables James and Philter and Sergeant Zemm, the fifth, Hoody. Hoody's bus was out in front so it was a logical conclusion that this was Hoody's acquaintance, there must have been a high surveillance compound camera outside the club. Lovely! Wonderful!

What mess was I in now?

At the top of the stairs I entered a small room down the hall, when Conan opened the door to it.

"After you, ma'am," whispered my newest associate, with false manners and a mock bow.

I ignored his jibe and entered unafraid, half expecting to be thrown into a cellar, half expecting to see Hoody sitting there with a broad grin on his face.

A solitary figure stood at the end of the room. I read tension on his back. The door closed and the person in question still hadn't turned around to address us. Conan, who was in fact having dinner returned to his meal, disregarding me once he turned me over to the alien in the corner.

"Why were you following us?" The question was asked so quietly, I barely registered that something was said, until Conan cleared his throat no doubt indicating that I should answer if I was expecting supper or even to get out of that room alive.

"You have to raise your voice if you want me to answer your question. I didn't hear you, the first time." I was not afraid of this man. I didn't know if I should be afraid but early on in my training I knew that it never helped much to be. It left one catatonic and unable to think at a time when thinking would be the only thing to save one's life.

The back straightened up and I could have sworn I heard a laugh coming from its direction. "Leave us," the back said.

To which Conan took up his napkin and left, closing the door softly behind my back.

The man stood with his back facing mine for so long, I eventually asked, "Is that you, Dimples?"

Still no answer.

"Never did get your name. Couldn't tell what it was from your signature. Your hand writing is crap by the way." I crept closer to his solitary figure.

If he was trying to be cool and mysterious, he was definitely accomplishing his goal and pissing me off at the same time. I was always to be held on a short leash when I was hungry, and I was famished.

I continued to close the distance between us by sauntering off to the side, trying to get the profile of the man. When I did, the profile I beheld instantly enlightened me of my folly. This was not Officer Dimples. This profile held a granite chiseled face and a clenched jaw, and he looked as mad as my teacher in the first grade when she discovered that I stuck chewing gum to her seat. Oh, boy, I was in trouble. Who was this man?

With haste my intellect overrode my stomach and I could think of nothing else but getting the hell out of there. Since he hadn't engaged me as yet in conversation, I began slinking away to the door in an attempt to escape. I thought maybe he wouldn't notice if I was gone.

The voice spoke again, "Don't bother. Francisco is standing outside the door."

Oh, I thought so Conan has a name? "Francisco?" I croaked, sounding out the name associated with my possible demise.

He turned without looking at me and said, "So, have you eaten? It must have been a long drive. Please be my guest, refresh yourself."

Suddenly, I was no longer hungry. I looked at the elaborate spread of food at the table as if it was poisoned.

As if reading my mind, he smiled as he invited me to partake, "I assure you it isn't poisoned or drugged."

To which I replied, "An assurance from a stranger, how reassuring"

Then he stepped out of the shadows, closed the distance between us both with six long strides, extended his hand palm upward and said, "Then let us not stand on ceremony. I am Christopher, this is my home. You are welcome."

Christopher:

Instantly taken aback, in person she was different to how she appeared on the office cameras. All I could think of was — damn, she too beautiful to be Police.

She was tall and slender like a model, brown curly hair, no, mahogany with dark, brown sun kissed highlights, pulled back into a single braid, delectably heart shaped lips, caramel brown skinned Goddess and oval shaped hazel brown eyes I could get lost in. Stunning.

Jane:
I didn't take his hand and I must have been staring at him as if I was stupid because he then invited me to, "Please have a seat."

It was my turn to be silent as I observed his face truly for the first time since our meeting. Once, while doing Greek mythology, I read about the gods and how they were immortalized in stone. Well, I felt as if one had come to life right in front of my eyes. However, I had to admit the full-on profile was even more daunting. I observed the only thing that softened his God like exterior was his chocolate brown eyes and his titanium blonde hair.

Then, it struck me. I had seen those eyes before. On Officer Dimples, of course! The two must have been related. I felt a little better knowing this.

"Wine?" he asked, lifting the wine bottle to pour, just like the perfect host.

"No, thank you," I casually replied as if we were old friends. I could've really done with a glass right about now but I had to keep my wits about me. I still didn't know why I was not allowed to leave for the moment, and I craved my freedom more than anything else in this world.

I was sensing if I played this casually, then I may avoid any impending disaster and so I compromised and said, "I would prefer some water, thank you."

Christopher casually switched to the water jug instead, as if he wasn't about to poison me a few moments ago, and poured some into my goblet until it was about three quarters full.

Too late, I suddenly realized that I had already given too much away. I confirmed my identity by asking about Officer Dimples, but I was not going to give anything else away. I was not going to plead, beg or ask, but I was ready to kick some butt if anyone stepped to me.

He handed me dishes and I took some food from each, not sure yet if I was going to eat any of it but I didn't want to raise the hackles on this one until I knew who or what I was dealing with. I was buying some quality thinking time and if pretending to be his dinner partner was the currency then I would do it.

So let me see…

This is what I read of the situation thus far, I followed Dimples, I was spotted, and Adonis… sorry, Christopher was not pleased that Dimples was followed. Hurt pride as to being tailed, but I was an officer of the law that was part of my job description. Or maybe, just maybe, these guys had a secret they didn't want me to know about, or a secret they were not sure how much I knew about, if anything at all.

I played with my food a bit, making sure not to mix the different dishes but pushing them from side to side. Without meeting his eye I observed Christopher who, like a scientist, was scrutinizing me from the other side of the table. Just as soon as he started to chew his food and swallow, I would follow suit.

Christopher smiled and began to eat. After twenty seconds I did the same but I was careful to only eat the dishes he ate.

"So, I understand it's your first time in the Neutral Zone?"

I was not about to enlighten Christopher about my itinerary or my movements. I looked into his adorable chocolate brown eyes and smiled with my eyes, but I kept my mouth full. It was bad manners to speak with one's mouth full. Besides, if this was going to be my last meal, I would enjoy it. These sautéed vegetables were really good. And that other thing was that butternut squash?

I could have sworn there was a twinkle in his eyes as he realized that I was defying him by refusing to answer his questions. Then he gave me an "I have all night" look and I genuinely became worried. I was never in a room with a man before and there were many other firsts that might occur tonight. There was a possibility that one of them could be my violation. We were taught at the Academy that this was a weapon of humiliation that men used when they couldn't get their way with women. The most effective torturing technique men had in their arsenals.

I casually commented, "I hope my car is safe out there."

Christopher assured me, "Your car is not the only thing that is safe here, Janey."

So he knew my name. "Just Jane please," then I paused trying to drain the panic from my voice, "well, if that is true, why am I not allowed to leave?"

Christopher gave a roaring laugh to this question. "I'm sorry, did I give you that impression? You are free to go whenever you like."

He was a bastard just like his blood relative. He knew that when he told me that Francisco was standing outside the door that I would interpret that to mean that he would stop me if I tried to leave.

It would seem that he believed that I was no longer a threat. Or so he wanted me to think.

I stood up and extended my hands remembering Superintendent Claudia's advice. "Well, dinner was lovely. Thank you for your hospitality and would you tell Dimples the drinks are on him the next time I'm in town?"

Christopher was already standing up when my hands were extended and instead of shaking my hand he gently swept his lips across the back of it and held it. I felt a flutter in the pit of my stomach and as if the temperature in the room had suddenly risen to forty degrees centigrade. Just like when I was sick but I wasn't sick now, was I?

Gesturing to the door with the other hand he said, "After you, Jane."

I took the hint. Although I wanted to run out of there, he held my hand until he opened my car door and said, "Parting is such sweet sorrow."

"I am sure it is, Christopher," I said, as he closed my car door.

As I pulled away from the curb, I thanked my lucky stars that I had my ten fingers and toes and that I could still wiggle them. By the time I reached the first set of traffic lights I realized that I was being tailed by a black Audi.

So, Christopher was returning the favour. A tail for a tail. What a gentleman, I thought contemptuously, a predatory gentleman.

CHAPTER 3

In an upper room, two men stood poised to engage in a heated debate, another man in silence, emitting cold anger.

"I told you, she knew nothing — she's new."

"You don't know that, Demetri."

"So stupid! How could you let her tail you to this address?"

"You don't know if she was tailing me, do you?"

"Demetri, for once get your head out of your ass! So, your face is pretty and women seem to follow you back to your lair without you asking them too. She is a cop! She could ruin our game here."

Christopher stepped out of the shadows and said, very nonchalantly despite his rage, "It looks as if I will be cleaning up your mess again, little brother." His statement proceeded a quantity of scotch being tossed down his throat to ease the knot between his shoulder blades.

CHAPTER 4

Christopher reclined in his mocha-coloured, double deluxe office recliner. To an onlooker it may have seemed like he was staring at the parker styled ceiling, probably inspecting a fault in the workmanship. But what Christopher was actually doing was holding onto his sanity by an extremely thin thread. He had not slept last night. Instead he had spent the last four hours gathering intel on last night's unexpected visitor. Where she lived, the people she worked with, her life's history, her future prospects and he was not a happy man.

He had lived in a world of conniving bitches, pseudo villains and quasi good guys. Long ago, he'd come to the conclusion that everyone was corruptible, compromised. He had never known a saint. Not even the Sisters who raised him at St. Stephens could be as squeaky clean as Janey. He was now foreseeing a problem with compromising her.

Oh Granddad's Bells! He was thinking of her as Janey again. Officer Parker, Officer Parker, Officer Parker. That was her name and he shouldn't forget it either, if he was to remain objective in the decisions that he would have to make.

Where was he? Yes, it would not only be near impossible to compromise the goodly officer but he was finding that he had to resist the urge not to do so.

When he decided to build this empire, he knew that he probably wouldn't get to heaven, not before he saw purgatory first. He had bribed too many officials, cut too many corners and made too many deals with the Mob. He never questioned what he had to do but now, for the first time in twenty years — since that time he got caught stealing Candy from Sister Bertha's jelly bean jar — he felt culpable, tarnished, and remorseful and another feeling he couldn't quite put his fingers on. He was having a hard time for what he knew he must do next.

Two hours later he was still staring at the file on his highly polished desk, with particular focus on the picture it contained. It was her recruitment picture. According to the date on her file, coupled with knowledge of her date of birth, he could guess that it was taken about eight and a half years ago. Her youthful, naïve, pixie face wasn't making matters easier for him.

This was ridiculous. He had Mob bosses eating out of his hands. He reassured himself that he was not having an attack of conscience. He would do what he always did; take care of business, because he had too. From his perspective, he had three options opened to him for now

(1) Compromise her and pay her off.

(2) Compromise her and recruit her, he could never have too many officers from the Androfemian territory working for him.

(3) Find out what she knew, who she told it to and get rid of her.

There, he had outlined a few choices… then why didn't he feel any better?

There was a knock proceeded by the opening of his office door. It was Francisco. "Hey boss. The bug sweep is over, we're clean, and the new girls are ready for inspection."

Christopher didn't attempt to render a reply, but Francisco had delivered his message so he closed the door quietly behind him.

CHAPTER 5

Demetri was a first-class pain in his ass, his neck, shoulders and about every other part of his anatomy but he never failed to keep their girls happy. And their enterprise had a lot of girls. Girls were his business. Girls made him rich, gave him control and influence over a lot of very important people. So no matter what his kid brother did to infuriate him, which was pretty much every maddening verb the dictionary could offer, he was in Demetri's debt.

Demetri flashed a smile to his older brother as he saw him entering the Ring room. There were four wrestling rings where the girls practiced every day. Demetri was their coach. He showed them what to wear, how to fight and how to look sexy doing it, so that their wealthy patrons wouldn't only enjoy themselves but that they would bet heavily and return for more.

This was just one of the many lucrative businesses that Christopher and his brother owned. And how could he not make a mint when he literally got the women for free and his patrons paid him a bundle for exclusivity? In return, he took care of the girls. Great medical plan, gorgeous facilities to reside in, beautiful chauffeur driven cars, exclusive shopping and a sizeable bonus when they left his employment. It was the perfect set up, except for the fact that it was as legal as bootlegging.

The women of Androfemur were always gorgeous, untouched and in demand. Of course, once they had frequented the Neutral Zone too often, they lost that innocent appeal they had about them, but he was not personally responsible for that. He had many kinds of girls — bartenders, wrestlers, valets, secretaries, spies, brides, actresses, drivers, dancers — but he never dealt with prostitutes professionally and rarely ever in a personal capacity. His girls were healthy and drug free and he, nor any of his men, had ever forced a girl to do a job she was uncomfortable with or did not agree to. His life as an orphan made him an empathetic supporter of Androfemur's less than upstanding citizens because he understood only too well what life could be like when the chips were down. The reality was he was saving these women from doing hard time in ill conditions and from being released without a penny to their names and no real prospects as ex-convicts of their State.

Francisco handed over the spectrum wand. This piece of equipment allowed him to read the implanted chips installed in every citizen of Androfemur. Every citizen of that territory, at birth, was installed with a nano chip behind her ear that allowed them to exist in that territory. As far as Christopher understood, exist was not a strong enough word, a person's life history was stored in that chip, everything from their place of birth, last known addresses, bank account balances, blood type, medical conditions, criminal convictions. He even heard that there was no way to make financial transactions without this chip, since the goodly citizens didn't handle money, only credit information stored on the chip. Christopher only used it to ensure the girls were in general good health before he had his doctor check them over and that there were no arrests for drug related charges. When the girls left his employment, a high-ranking banking official of Androfemur who Christopher had on his payroll credited the girls' accounts so it could be readable on their chips. The wand was acquired from a client who happened to be the Commissioner of Prisons.

But that was not the only function of the wand. The wand also temporarily disabled any possible transmissions. Officially there was only a linear function to the girls' nano chips but his tech guys discovered that the application was only limited by the user and not the manufacturer, leaving a very real possibility of the chips being remotely activated to spy on the host and their location.

Had it come down to it, he could have used this on Jane Parker last night but there was no way to get a reading unless he held her down to use it. Besides he learned she was a cop from Demetri before he met her acquaintance and that was all he really needed to know. After meeting the officer in person last night he was pretty sure she would never allow him to get that information unless it was over her dead body. He did not allow her five-feet seven inches frame, her cool hazel eyes and her general good manner to fool him. Even before he read her file and discovered that after the first three years of her initial training, she worked at the Androfemur's Training Academy (ATA), as one of their Martial Arts instructors, he read her instinctively like tea leaves. The way she stepped lightly on the balls on her feet, the position she took when she entered the room, the fact that she never let her fear show, he had a strong suspicion she could handle herself in a fight.

Christopher was sure he could take her but then he liked his women willing and pliable. He never had to force a woman to get anything he wanted and he was not about to start now. He was no Demetri but he definitely got the family gene for charming women and he used it when he had to. He wasn't sure what happened last night though. Maybe Janey was immune to his brand of charm. He couldn't say that thought made him feel good about himself but it told him something — if the fish wasn't biting then he would have to use different bait.

After the inspection, Christopher left Demetri with the girls and returned to his office. Maybe he was going about this the wrong way entirely. Maybe he needed to find out the desires of Jane Parker's heart. Just maybe whatever it was, he could make her an offer she couldn't refuse. He learned in his business that everybody had a price, but the catch was that it might not be in dollars, cents or credit. He just had to find out what Janey's price was. He smiled for the first time that day. First he couldn't allow her to leave the territory without making his offer. He looked at the wall clock. It was six a.m. and a honeyed sunlight glow was streaming through his opened windows. He got on the phone again to a very influential client, on his private number.

"Good morning, Frank."

CHAPTER 6

Jane:

At the exchange, she counted two women. Where were the others? Her orders were to collect five women at the Midwalk point. After last nights' experience all she wanted to do was to get the hell out of the Neutral Zone. She took out her mobile ear plugs and connected to Superintendent Claudia's office.

Superintendent Claudia reiterated her order in a not too pleasant voice over the phone. "You are to collect five women who will be released in your custody." Then she repeated the "five women" part as if I was impaired. She also added, if the situation had not sorted itself out by the end of the day, that I was to hunt down (those were her words not mine) the other three and bring them back to the territory.

Almost forty-eight hours after entering into the Neutral Zone, the only thoughts on my mind were, these incompetent buffoons, how could they misplace three women? One misplaced a side of an earring not a released prisoner.

I had spent all day yesterday and most of today on the phone, driving around the Neutral Zone with the rest of the day shift in an attempt to track the whereabouts of the three prisoners who were now in breach of the Immigration laws of the Neutral Zone and the Nuuk Convention between the two territories. None of them had any written permission or permits to be there. This inadvertently made my problem an even bigger one.

The Maledrome border patrol said they only received two women. The Neutral Zone officers said they handed over five women to them. Eventually, when I got a look at the release forms, I discovered that the officer Sergeant Cotswold who signed receiving five women couldn't be located at the moment. But those weren't the words used. His superiors said that he was indisposed which I understood to mean, they couldn't account for his whereabouts. Further investigations revealed that he was on vacation leave for the next three months as of yesterday to an unknown destination in the Maledrome district. A district I had as much access to as a man would have to the Androfemian district. Lovely! I wanted to scream and curse out someone, anyone, the Cotswold guy for not being there, the stupid Maledrome Border Patrol Administration for not insisting on having a vacation destination and contact number on record. Not that the information was going to be of any use to me but the Maledrome border patrol officers might have been able to contact him, the genius staff sergeant who apparently could not read the transfer sheet nor count up to five!

This was a nightmare of impossible proportions. On one end I was being stonewalled by the Maledrome border patrol. It was a hunch of course and one that I could not prove. At the other end I was the recipient of Superintendent Claudia's biting sarcasm. So much for my promotion.

I released a sigh of frustration. I felt bad because all my fellow officers were so helpful, taking me on all my inquiries and basically allowing me access to any equipment I needed.

I just wanted to punch something but they were all so nice. I had to get out of there before I took my frustration out on the undeserving. As I stood, I looked up and saw a familiar face penetrating the rays of light through the entrance of the building. It was Francisco. He was searching the office space until he locked eyes onto me and moved forward like a heat seeking missile.

I thought I had seen the last of him for good. What did he want? Whatever it was, I had not a moment to spare. Apparently not even for lunch, my stomach growled. I was tired, hungry and frustrated and in no mood for conversation, especially with his kind. I was beginning to realize that the Separation must not have occurred soon enough for women.

When he came closer, I whispered through bared teeth, "What do you want?"

Francisco looked grim when he said, "The boss wants to have a word."

Turning my back to him, and busying my hands by attempting to straighten the desk I had on loan, I barked out, "I'm busy!"

I could see a card between Francisco's fore and middle fingers. I contemplated if I should let him stand there with his fingers stuck out forever. Then I realized that I was being petulant because I was hungry and irritable, which was not at all professional. I approached the front desk where he stood and I snatched the white and gold card from his fingers. There was a note scribbled in black ink on the back of it. It read, *I might know where your girls are. Chris.*

CHAPTER 7

Jane:

I must say that sitting next to Christopher at the back of his town car, in such close proximity, was a bit disconcerting. I could see the rise and fall of his chest and his breathing was audible, although to the trained eye and ear — it was barely perceptible. Sitting next to him made me aware of him and I can't say I liked it very much. It made me aware of myself and this made me feel very uncomfortable.

For some reason he sat in the middle seat while I occupied the next seat, closer to the door. I was about to ask him to move around when I notice his briefcase was taking up the other third of the seat. So, I did the best I could do to straighten up, minimizing the space between us, which had the effect of me looking like if I was trying not to melt into the door.

"Comfortable?" he asked. All I could come up with was a little plastic smile, which disappeared the minute he turned front again to signal something to Francisco.

"So," I announced. "Talk." I had no intention of being brief but I really couldn't trust my voice to say any more, sitting so close to him.

He smiled sensually and said, "More haste, less speed my Janey."

I wanted to tell him to go fuck himself, that I was not his Janey, or anybody else's for that matter, but I was desperate for the information he said he had. It was a mystery to me that he knew about the girls' disappearance at all. Then I had a thought. Maybe officer Dimples informed him of my predicament. I belatedly found out Demetri Mac Pherson, his brother, was an officer of the Neutral Zone Correctional Facilities.

"You hungry?" Christopher asked.

"Why are you always trying to fatten me, are you eyeing me for the kill?" I was on the scoreboard again, at least. My stomach was not controlling my thinking.

There it was again, that slow sexy smile. Christopher must have known that I really hated him right about now; people say I have a face like an opened book and I wasn't holding anything back.

I had no patience to bolster egos today, I was in my play pen, doing my job, playing by my rules.

He replied, as if he didn't acknowledge my last comment. "Actually, I am on my way to lunch. You would have to sit and watch me finish since I never discuss business over the most substantial meal of the day."

"Here's a thought. What about giving me the information now? Then you can go off to lunch or whatever else you're up to."

"You're just a bit impatient, aren't you?" he indicated the bit part with his two well-manicured and very long fingers.

"What I am is 'working', apparently you are just full of hot air, and wasting my time." I quickly opened the door and was making a hasty retreat, when those hands — which by the way were very strong — clenched my wrist.

He spoke coolly as if I wasn't about to dismiss him two seconds ago. "I know where they are and if you do as I ask, you will have them released into your custody tomorrow morning."

My body was rigid, halfway inside, halfway outside the vehicle. Did I even dare believe this man, Christopher? Suddenly I remembered all the things Superintendent Claudia said about men, how they were not to be trusted and all the things my aunt had said, and what pretty much every Androfemian citizen believed about men. There must have been some grain of truth in it. After all where there was smoke someone was definitely in violation of code 4.

I didn't know if I trusted him to do as he said but right now I had no leads and no one else was helping me out. So, I reluctantly sat back down. I asked the obvious. "I'm getting the feeling you aren't doing this out of the goodness of your heart."

His smile told me what I needed to know. He wanted something. So I came right out and asked, "What do you want?"

He replied noncommittally. "Some of your time... for starters."

I would do what he asked but he would respect me. I didn't have a piece of trump in my hand but that in no way left me handicapped.

"Listen Christopher," I began with an acidic tone. "Here is what is going to happen. I will give you until nine thirty pm tonight, not tomorrow, to return my charges unharmed to the Maledrome Midwalk Point. During this "time" that I spend with you, there will be no monkey business. We will talk, and there will be absolutely no touching. Starting with you putting that briefcase between us and sitting on the other side of it." I didn't want to look at him when I said that final piece, but now I turned sideways to face him to reinforce this point.

"Your driver will return me to this compound before nine thirty p.m. unharmed, with my three charges," the three I emphasized by putting up my right hand with my fore, middle and index fingers extended, "and I will leave the Neutral Zone with no unforeseen occurrences. Do we agree?"

I don't know why I said that but I suddenly realized that I was dealing with a heavy weight because if he could accomplish what he claimed he could do, then he had a lot more clout than I expected. From my research, I knew he was a huge businessman in the community but if his tentacles extended into the public sector then he was definitely not to be underestimated.

Christopher then said, coolly, "You ask for an awful lot but give very little in return, Jane."

"The way I see it is you ask for the restriction of my personal freedom for something that is rightly mine. And… We are yet to make a deal, sir."

Christopher knew I called him on his crap and he knew I was dead serious, he said, "Deal," flashing his white smile and perfect lips, he extended his left hand towards me for a handshake.

"I said, no touching," I reminded him where he and I stood or sat if one wanted to be literal.

He gallantly removed his suitcase from the end window seat and placed it in a compartment, in the side door.

I sighed; this was going to be a long afternoon.

CHAPTER 8

Janey had ignored Christopher's presence for most of the way to his Restaurant on the Upper Western Side of the Neutral Zone. He gathered from their little talk that all she wanted to do was to go home and becoming more important to him at the moment, to get away from him. He was beginning to suspect that Demetri was correct all along, she really didn't know anything about their set up. She seemed to be more preoccupied with not sitting too close to him and she refused to give him any eye contact. Janey must have been a real badass on Androfemur, but she was shy. This intrigued Christopher, not because she was keeping her distance though. He pretty much knew that the women of Androfemur under a particular age were inexperienced virgins when it came to men. What he admired was her courage.

To begin with, she got into a car with two men she barely knew. They could be taking her anywhere and in a place like the Neutral Zone, her body could turn up anywhere in the district or not. Nevertheless, that didn't seem to particularly bother her. She dictated her own terms through their negotiations quite tactically, although he held most of the cards. He had a hunch that if her back was against the wall she would fight him like an alley cat. He looked across at her stubborn chin sticking out and had no choice but to be in awe of the huge pair of balls on her.

His plans for her were simple; he already got the information he needed from her. She was not a threat. There was no offer to be made, that would only raise her suspicions. Christopher was looking forward to a nice long afternoon with very desirable female companionship. He knew that he would enjoy looking at her because he was already doing so even though she was wearing those dreadful blue-grey work pants and navy-blue blouse. He would get her out of those as soon as practicably possible. Maybe Jane didn't know this, but there was a lot a man could do even if he was not allowed to touch. After all, he was in the business of awakening other men's desires through observation of the female anatomy. There will be no touching but he intended to do a lot of looking… at least for the moment.

CHAPTER 9

Jane:

This is stupid. I could have sworn Christopher didn't look too upset when the waiter spilled red wine on my blouse. Now I was forced to sit in this cubicle while he got an outfit from one of his nearby stores. Although I insisted that my blouse was fine albeit ruined, Christopher was playing the gallant hero.

I was not sure why he really wanted to have me around. He must be really starved for female company especially with the "no touching" rules I enforced. I deduced that for a man of his caliber he was should have been accustomed to more willing female company in the Neutral Zone but maybe, that was the kick of the entire thing. I was not exactly eager.

If there was a game that he was playing, I would win. Armed with the limited knowledge of our previous encounters it was doubtless that he was smiling all the while at my discomfort. Well, two could play that game. As of now I would be the most delightful airhead he'd ever met. That would really throw him off and extract his joy with a syringe. I laughed to myself in the confines of the cubicle covered with an intricate twentieth century Chinese lilac and jade floral design. If there was nothing else I could admire about Christopher, and there was so much when you really examined it objectively, he had really great taste when it came to décor. His restaurants, his cars, they were all so, well, so pretty. I myself could only be described as functional and, with the exception of my BMW which was the finest machine ever created on God's green earth, I never gave much thought to beauty on a whole. That made me sort of an odd ball on Androfemur, a territory frothing with delicate blooms, rich hues, clean beautifully decorated streets and let's not forget, females that were born with a natural sense of style. Somehow that gene skipped me. Whatever he did, I hoped Christopher wouldn't bring a dress.

I jumped, startled as several heavy leather garment bags were placed over the top of the cubicle door. I opened the door to thank whoever dropped them off but whoever it was disappeared like a ninja into the black of night.

Opening the bags one by one I examined their contents. He had to be kidding. No way was I wearing any of those skimpy threads. In a state of undress, I sat in the cubicle fortified only in my underwear.

I started to call out for someone to return the prodigal wine stained blouse. "Hello, hello, is there anyone there?"

After shouting at the top of my lungs for ten minutes, no one answered. Fine. I grabbed up the first garment bag wrapped it around my torso and marched outside. My bravado left me when I got to the kitchen door; I peered through and called the first person which happened to be a graying gentleman dressed in white to come to my assistance. Leaving a crack in the door I explained that I needed to see Christopher immediately, that it was of the utmost importance.

Approximately three minutes later, I heard a male baritone voice outside my cubicle. "What seems to be the trouble, dear?"

CHAPTER 10

Oh, Christopher knew what the problem was. He instructed the maître that he sent over to his stores on the sizes of the shoes, outfits, colors, styles and he insisted... only dresses. Christopher wanted to see her in a dress. Now she was kicking up a fuss, no doubt something or everything about the outfits outraged her sensibilities. He wished he had Demetri here to coax her into anything he wished her to wear. He smiled at the thought of him wishing his brother was here to deal with a virginal woman. Then he belatedly reminded himself, a woman who was a very intelligent and determined cop.

"The trouble is, I am not wearing any of these THINGS you got from your store. They are ridiculously revealing. What kind of store do you own anyway?" she shouted in exasperation over the cubicle door.

"Come on, Janey, I am sure they are not that bad, I saw the outfits myself they are pretty decent by my standards," he replied encouragingly.

The double doors of the cubicle swung opened vigorously hitting the sides of the walls.

"This is what you call decent?" she hissed.

Jane Parker opened the door wearing the burgundy, velvet, off the shoulder dress, whose hem was closely snug to her thighs and neckline revealed round, ripe, delicious breast. She was perfect. Only then he realized that the game he was playing was a dangerous one because now he desperately wanted to see, feel and taste what was beneath the dress.

Christopher unconsciously swallowed, then suggested, "That was the worst one. Try the black one, there are sleeves on that one and the skirt seems to cover up more."

She dropped her clenched fist to her sides and marched into the cubicle.

A brief time later, she interrupted his thoughts, as he hadn't realize that she changed in quick time, returning to continue her fashion show. "Is this your idea of decent? A plunging neckline and virtually no back?"

"Jane, I need you to trust me. Can you do that?" his request was a plea.

However, Jane replied with pouted lips, "No."

"Please, Janey."

She seemed to consider his entreaty as she sat on the chair outside the cubicle. She bent her torso and covered her face with her hands, now he witnessed her shoulders shaking. Was she... was she crying? He stepped forward and regretfully sat next to her.

"Janey, I am sorry, Janey." He was pleading with her now because he felt as if his heart was breaking watching this Venus in black break down.

"Please don't cry darling." Christopher put her covered face on his chest and stroked her hair. She felt so good in his arms, she fit right into them as if she belonged there. Her warm, ragged breath was jerky now... but her escaped breaths had a musical tone to it, she was not crying...

She uncovered her face which was red by now and revealed her white teeth and uncontrollable laughter.

"This designer needs to be shot, but you are correct it is the most decent of all the outfits and the shoes are kind of pretty. It reminds me of back home," she added in a wistful tone. "Can you pass the shoes, they are in the bag," she requested. He got up searched the bag and returned.

Why would he think that a girl like Jane would cry over a fashion faux pas? She goaded him when they first met and laid down the law in his car. A silly dress would certainly make her laugh. She was so beautifully brave. Instead of handing over the shoes, he knelt unfastening the laces of her work shoes and slipped the pearl covered heels onto her feet, noting her delicate arched instep. He was not deaf to the sharp intake of her breath as he deliberately made eye contact while he slipped on the other side. His groin ached as he felt his manhood stiffen.

Clearly she was affected, there was no denying it. But he had been having sex since he was fifteen years old and he had never experienced anything so intimate in his entire thirty-three years. He felt as if he was slowly undressing her instead of putting on her shoes. He knew it was a perilous game he was playing and yet there was no stopping himself. He intended to enjoy her company and extract as much enjoyment from doing so but cautioned himself as it dawned on him that the hunter was quickly becoming the hunted. He felt as if he was being squeezed by a python but he didn't want to escape. Reason niggled at him and he knew he would have to quit whilst he was ahead. He told himself that as soon as she was out of his orbit, he would forget her and to ensure it, he would ask Demetri to find him a willing girl to come to his bed that night.

Good call girls were hard to find in the Neutral Zone and he was encouraged every day to do something about it but he refused all business arguments put forward by his would-be clientele. The Mob bosses chided him. It came down to the same reason every time, someone else was making the money he could be pocketing himself, and his answer was always the same, let them, he was already rich.

He had a ready access to the best girls in the region everyone knew that. This was the reason why he had the best girls none of them were into prostitution or drugs. He reasoned there was a definite correlation between having the best girls and staying out of the prostitution game. Besides, he rarely ever was in need of one, not when he was one of the region's most eligible bachelors. But he would have to try to forget Jane quickly, and the sooner the better.

As he guided her back through the kitchen doors, everyone stopped to stare. The kitchen staff, the waiting staff and the guest who were beautifully outfitted in tailor made suits and dresses. Everyone was staring. He was the owner and usually he was the center of attention which was always unwanted. Today everyone was looking at Jane and, no doubt, cursing his good fortune.

CHAPTER 11

It took all of my martial arts and police training to keep my back erect and eyes straight ahead. Christopher was leading me into the dining area and his left hand was on the center of my back, leaving a scorching effect that seemed to be burning through the layers of my skin. I felt my face going red, the heat staining my cheeks. My body was hot and cold at the same time as I felt my nipples harden under the fabric of the dress. The walk of shame was over as I realized we neared a private dining alcove. No doubt they all thought I was his new paramour. Little did they know I was the cop he was blackmailing into having lunch and possibly dinner later on with him, the very same cop who insisted on the no touching rule that he was flagrantly disregarding.

As soon as we got into the alcove, I stepped away from his touch. Quickly, I pulled out my own chair in case he used this activity as an excuse to touch my back again. I resolved that he would not guess at my discomfort as a result of his contact. My body was doing strange things. My breathing was perceptible, my stomach was doing summersaults, my lips were parted and my underwear was wet. And as much as it all made me feel uncomfortable, it made me feel doubly excited. As if that emotion was not enough to deal with, I was angry that he defied my no touching rule twice. I identified that as being the cause of my altered state in this instance. I surmised as long as I kept out of his reach, I would be able to think straight and come out of this one on top.

CHAPTER 12

She sank slowly into her seat and tossed her mahogany colored hair over her shoulders. An image of her on top, riding him slowly flashed across Christopher's mind. Oh, he definitely wanted to see her on top of him, her dripping wet cunt sliding smoothly and strongly over his...

"What are we having today, sir, ms?"

The waitress interrupted his descent into pornography. He was associated with the most sort after women in the region, models, stars and he never day dreamed about any of them naked in a public restaurant. What was this woman doing to him? If he was honest with himself, she had hexed him since the first night they met; he did spend a long time gazing at her picture in her file. He really had to call Demetri as soon as lunch was over.

"Something hot and fast. What about you?" she asked him in an innocent tenure.

"The unusual Melanie, by two and a bottle of Chandelier." he heard himself answer slowly and deliberately.

His thoughts were still raking over her last response, "Hot and fast," when she said, "So you must be either well known or you know the staff pretty well in this place, for them to be at your beck and call like that."

He locked onto her eyes and watched them change from a soft hazel to a dark stormy version. She looked away briefly, then occupied herself by picking up the water goblet in front of her. She took a sip from it.

At least there was some progress, she refused to eat or drink anything the night they met until he had partaken of it first. This was a good sign, and whether she wanted to admit it or not, her defenses were falling.

"Something like that," he answered without giving too much away.

She already knew that he fully and part owned about seventy businesses including this restaurant *Star Fish*. He was a bachelor who usually kept to himself which made him more sort after and one of the most eligible in the Neutral Zone. After her unlawful detention she used "APHID" (accessed, personal historical information and documents) to access everything she could find on Christopher MacPherson. His businesses seemed to be all above board but she knew that no one got that high up being squeaky clean, not in this environment of notorious backstabbers. But she didn't care, she just wanted her prisoners released into her custody and to lie on the clean blue sheets of her own bed.

There was a long silence at their table until she said. "I guess that's how you usually like your company?"

"Pardon me?"

"Dressed in revealing clothes from one of your stores, quietly seated at one of your restaurants, waiting for you to address them" she asked, goading him again.

"If I did, I certainly wouldn't have asked your lovely self to accompany me to lunch."

"Touché, MacPherson"

"Looks like someone has been doing her homework," he inquired, testing the wine that was brought to their table.

"Yes, informative and, I'm afraid, imperative reading. Especially after one has been forcefully invited to dine with an unknown companion," she replied

"I am glad to know the adjective was unknown and not unpleasant. Somehow that knowledge has made my day." He smiled, really enjoying their banter.

"Oh, I doubt very much. Today is yet another day and you have again elicited another blackmailed meal with me. Makes me wonder what the special is in this place, and what poison you may have laced it with this time."

"Oh, come now, Janey, your imagination is in hyper drive. Besides, poison is not my apparatus of torture." There was his sexy smile again.

"Please do tell, enlighten an ignorant subject as to what your arsenal of instruments contain. I might learn a thing or two yet," she countered.

He knew that she was angry, to be held against her will waiting on information that he already had. Her eyes were stormy and dark, her lips were moistened and delectable. He felt his groin muscle tighten and added, "I am sure the weapons in your arsenal are not only primed but effective, Janey." He himself was being tortured slowly and he was enjoying it else he would just make a phone call and have her charges released into her custody. But something told him he would never see her again and that was a torture he was unwilling to contemplate at the moment.

His unexpected complement made her blush. Stupid man, she wanted to get up and walk away right now and tell him shove his information into Pluto's hole, but he was her best lead. Besides he agreed that he would take care of it and she would be leaving the Neutral Zone tonight at nine thirty p.m. with her charges, so she had, what, seven hours in his presence? She unconsciously checked her wrist watch confirming her prognosis, then her eyes returned to his.

"You couldn't be bored of the chit chat already, Janey?"

"I am sure you pay the women you know to say otherwise, but I do have more exciting things on my mind."

"Like what?"

She was stuck. She had nothing in mind, so instead of being caught in a lie she said the first thing that came to her mind. "I have my comfortable sheets waiting on me back home, if you must know." She rolled her eyes at her lack of originality.

"If it's bed you are thinking of I have several very comfortable ones. You are most welcomed to any of them," he offered.

She spurted out a little of the water she had in her mouth and choked on the rest.

He was at her side within seconds. "Are you OK?" he whispered gently, stroking her exposed back very smoothly.

That was all she needed burnt into her mind, an image of herself in his bed. Christopher slowly taking off her clothes, looking into her eyes the same way as he was when he put on those shoes a few minutes ago. Her pussy lips were leaking again, with every stroke of his fingertips as if he was stroking her there. She weakened then shivered at his touch.

"Christopher?" she asked, shakily measuring her voice.

"What darling?" he whispered ever so gently.

"I need to lie down, I don't feel so good," she complained.

"OK, let's wrap this up, and I will take you somewhere safe," he replied.

"A hospital bed will be fine," she insisted.

"I'll take you to my apartment it's close by and I will have a doctor there in no time." He lifted her, cradling her in his arms, out of the restaurant and into his town car.

CHAPTER 13

Jane:

It had to be the food or the wine. I was getting hot flashes, feeling cold, my stomach had butterflies, my vagina was pulsing and I was feeling weak. However, Christopher tried to deny it, he definitely tried to poison me or slip me something. I cradled his neck as he slid me into the car. I drifted off into a sensual daydream as he continued to stroke my hair. His proximity felt comforting but I was definitely not feeling any relief of the symptoms.

My drawers were soaked right through now and I could feel tiny convulsions in my abdominal region. It was getting worse.

CHAPTER 14

Jane:

That doctor was silly. She said that I was fine and that Mr. Mac Pherson would help me if I would let him, afterward the symptoms would leave. Was Christopher a doctor? How could he help me? She was the doctor and she couldn't help me. If this is what passed for doctoring in the Neutral Zone, the citizens were in a lot of trouble.

After the doctor left, Christopher entered the room and the symptoms intensified as Christopher stroked my forehead.

"The doctor said you will be fine, sweetheart."

"You are doing this to me, aren't you?" I surmised, not knowing the answer for sure, but only just realizing that the symptoms were intensifying every time Christopher got closer, especially when he touched me.

"Doing what?" he asked

"Yes, making me feel this way. The symptoms seem to intensify when you are around especially when you are touching me like you are now."

Christopher cleared his throat. "You want to tell me what the symptoms are, Janey?" he whispered, quietly putting his weight on the mattress.

"It's kind of embarrassing, so no," I announced decidedly.

"Do you want to feel better?" he inquired in earnest.

"Yes, I have work this evening and it makes no sense carrying on like this if I could get rid of this feeling. The doctor said some foolishness about you helping me."

"OK, then tell me, Janey, I'm listening," he whispered, focusing on her lips.

"Well, my head feels like it is swarming, a kind of disorientation."

"And?"

"And my stomach has butterflies in it."

"And?"

"I feel like I have a fever, especially in the pit of my stomach, but my chest feels..." I looked away.

"Go on," Christopher encouraged.

"My chest feels cold."

"Your chest feels hot and cold at the same time?"

"Yes, inside my chest feels like it is on fire and my... my... breast, my nipples feel cold. Well it's more like they are behaving as they would if they were cold."

CHAPTER 15

Christopher buried his face in her hair and groaned out loud, laughing to himself, then asked again, "What else anything else, darling? Don't you leave anything out even if it is really personal or embarrassing, I promise I won't laugh again, I want to help you."

"Well there is a discharge... you know down there, I'm wet..."

He could take it no longer. He groaned aloud again, stifling the sound in her hair.

When she looked up at him, his chocolate brown eyes were raging as if he were in a predicament.

"Janey?"

"Yes."

"The doctor was right."

"Oh," she said as if confused. "Right about what?"

"About the symptoms being only temporary and going away."

"Was she right about you helping me... you know... get rid of it?"

"I think I could help."

"Well what are you waiting for then, help me!" she demanded.

He groaned softly again. This time it sounded like a whimper, "I can't, sweetheart."

She was angry. She thundered, "Why the hell not? You said you wanted to help!"

"I also made you a promise."

"And what promise is that?"

"That I would not touch you."

"You have been breaking that promise all afternoon."

Christopher quickly withdrew his hands as if he only just noticed that the accusation was true. "This is a different kind of touching Janey, the kind you do when you are taking a shower."

"So you mean I could take a shower and that might help?"

"It might, or it could get worse."

"Will you help then?"

Christopher cleared the frog that was in his throat and returned an answer in a husky baritone voice. "You are going to have to trust me and allow me to do things that no one has ever done to you before. Are you willing to take that chance?"'

Jane Parker was silent for a really long time as if considering the offer. "OK, let's do it, I have a very high tolerance for pain."

"What about pleasure?"

"Huh?" she asked innocently.

"Nothing. Ah... remember when I said that it would be like when you were taking a shower?"

"I remember."

"Well you would need to be undressed as if you were in the shower."

And he stood there without turning around until she said "Surely you don't expect me to get undressed in front of you?"

"Janey, I am going to touch you in a few minutes. Surely it should not matter."

"Can't you touch me under the sheets? Without looking, I mean."

"I will try my hardest not to look, but at a certain point it may be impossible not to."

"OK, when we come to that bridge, we will cross it, turn around."

So, Christopher turned around and chuckled, then instantly sobered. He was a beast; he should be charged and hung without a trial. He was going to make Janey cry out and cum. He had no right to touch her, but when she asked him to, so sweetly, so innocently, how could he say no? He had been dreaming of being inside her all afternoon long and although he had no intention of going all the way, he was going to allow himself this sweet torture. He would hear her cry out and watch her while she did it. It was all he had any right to. Besides, it served him right to be denied her dripping wet… Oh, he did not want to think too much of her naked body underneath those cream silk sheets.

"OK, I am ready, you can turn around now." Like a lamb to the slaughter she had no clue as to what he was going to do and most likely she would be frightened out of her wits. He had to reassure her.

"Janey, I need you to trust me and allow me to…"

"Get on with it, Christopher, I am not made of glass. I won't break."

His face got closer to hers now and he gently whispered. "Yes you will, over and over again." As he said these words, he sat to the side of the bed his lips descended onto her surprised ones. He tasted her and coaxed her mouth open, then he tasted her tongue, very softly caressing the inside of her mouth, whilst his trembled. She tasted like wine, grapes, chocolate and all the sweet things a boy desires to have when he was a kid. A moan escaped from her lips. He allowed his hand to drift slowly beneath the sheets, stroking the sides of her breast, then circling her nipples. They were hard like granite against her creamy soft breast. His groin tightened even more when he thought that he was the one that turned her on like that, even against her own will.

His mouth replaced his hands on her breast, his tongue slowly circling the tips, his mouth covering the entire globe sucking it strongly, softly and slowly. He stopped to look at her face. She was biting her lips. her eyes were closed shut.

When he stopped she opened her eyes.

"It would be better that whatever you are feeling you scream it out. I won't think less of you if you do, Janey." He took her hands that were clinched at her sides and placed them on his head. "That's better"

This turn of events surprised her a bit but she promised she would let him help her. He started his assault again, on her lips this time, surer, swifter, more demanding.

She cried out, then said, "I'm sorry."

He laughed and then encouraged her by saying, "It gets rid of the symptoms faster."

"Why didn't you say that before? I've been holding back."

He laughed really loud at her reply. "What? Did I say something funny?"

"No, darling, you were perfect." he plunged inside of her mouth, this time she allowed him to, freely taking his tongue into her mouth and moaning once again. Christopher was not sure how much more he could take of her moaning without driving himself completely insane, and possibly into her, but he promised if he felt himself going there, he would run away from her grasp and his house without so much as looking back.

She pushed up her breast to him, inviting him to suck on it again. Suck he did. He took her into his mouth as he wanted her to take him into her mouth, and mirrored the motions he saw in his head of her sucking his cock. She screamed out and trembled, "Oh, God, No!"

"Honey, what's wrong?"

"Christopher, you promised me you would make me feel better. What's going on?"

"I promise, Janey, if you do as I ask, it will go away in a few more minutes. Patience my angel."

"OK."

"Take my hand and show me where it hurts the most."

She swiftly took his hands to under her breast in the region of her heart. He softened at her expression when she did this. He imagined she was telling him that her heart was hammering. Then she moved his hand away from her heart, and directed him reluctantly in the region of her lower abdomen.

He had to restrain himself, otherwise he would burst. He then said in a controlled voice, "Janey, whatever I do, I need you to keep looking at me. I will not hurt you." He said this, but his face was red, his jugular veins straining for control and his eyes stormy.

"OK," she replied, more confused than ever. He seemed to be just as afraid as she was, but she found that she wanted to trust him.

He took her hand, covered it with his and lead her down to her wet spot; she jumped a little when he made contact. She was very, very, wet and pulsating. Her cunt was like a dripping faucet and his job was to stop the leak. He loved his job so much.

"Janey ?"

"Yes," she answered in a hoarse voice.

"I need you to keep looking at me while I help you, OK?"

She did not reply, but looked up at him, biting down on her lips. She looked so sexy now. He slipped his middle finger into her cunt and her vaginal lips closed over his finger in welcome. He was losing control in his own pants. Slowly, he slipped in two fingers, she was instinctively moving with the rhythm of his fingers, biting down on her lips and looking at him with those steamy grey eyes, and God bless her soul, she never took her eyes off of him unless it was to scream, "Oh God" or "More". Instead of the release he expected, her passion was mounting and mounting, as she screamed for more and more. They both were being tortured alive. She wanted to cum and there were only two ways she could do that. He could fuck it out of her or he could suck it out of her.

He chose the latter. No doubt it was in an attempt to continue to torture himself but he had already taken enough liberties with Jane Parker. Besides, he promised that he would not hurt her and the latter would give him the certitude and, maybe later, absolution from the act he was about to commit.

He pulled back the sheets to reveal her blushing, luscious caramel brown body. My God, she was without a doubt the most gorgeous woman he had ever seen. He continued to keep eye contact to give her reassurance. But as soon as he placed his lips on her engorged dripping labia, he knew he should have run when he had the chance. She tasted of honey, no, wild nectar and he could not get enough of her. His tongue circled

74

her clitoris, his tongue plunged into her corridors of joy, his tongue drank from her fountain.

She cried out all kinds of profanity, "Fuck, Fuck," "God No", while she trashed about in his bed, until her body arched to the ceiling as if it would break then lowered unto the cool sheets as she found the release she sought.

His face was mysterious. That was the first thing she noted, when she descended from the clouds, he was upset, and his eyes were tempestuous.

"What's wrong, Christopher? Did I do something wrong?"

"No, honey, you were great."

"I feel a whole lot better, so you must have done something right." As she said this, he turned his back and was walking out the door.

"Hey, now I know something is wrong." Jane jumped out of his bed with the sheets wrapped around her, matching his walking speed.

"You OK?" she asked, touching his face intimately.

He joked and added, "I am not too well myself, Janey."

"You didn't tell me what I had was contagious, I never wanted to make you sick; you have to believe me. Maybe I could help you," she said, catching his left hand as he placed the other one on the door to escape.

"I seriously doubt that," he added in mocking laughter.

"Why? Because you know what to do, and I don't? Well I'm sure you could talk me through it, you know, tell me what to do." she said in a hopeful tone.

"I'll get someone else to help, it would be less complicated."

She let go of his left hand. He left the apartment, shutting the door firmly behind him.

He never returned.

Ten minutes later, Francisco came to her door to take her back to the Outpost. There, to her surprise, she discovered her charges waiting, she looked at the time. It was only six p.m., the transport was outside and she could finally go home.

So, why was she feeling so lost in facing the prospect of Androfemur? Why was it that all she could think of was... was Christopher's tongue, on her skin, in her mouth, inside of her? She blushed and walked with her charges, chaining them to the bars on the prison transport.

CHAPTER 16

Jane:

Today is Tuesday the 20th of June, 2079, a day I had been dreading for nearly two months. Today, I would return to the Neutral Zone and try to establish contact with him.

Christopher MacPherson, the man who not only knowingly tricked me into committing an unspeakable act but who now according to the E.B.P.B, was also a criminal. The last part of which I was to establish by gathering evidence about his operation which entailed me returning to the Neutral Zone, undercover of course. Well, I suspected Superintendent didn't really mean the undercover so much since he already knew I was a cop, but under his covers in his bed if necessary to nail Christopher. I was not looking forward to deceiving him or anyone else. Undercover work was not my forte. I always found lying extremely taxing as I had an extremely expressive face. Besides, everyone I knew told me I was a bad liar.

I dreaded today because I doubted my abilities to carry out my duty for the first time. Also, I would have to face Christopher again, something I never intended to do after I discovered what he did to me was considered to be a "sexual act" and that I was now soiled according to the Superintendent, which proved to be useful to the organization but bad news for my reputation, if it ever got out.

After I returned and completed post operation briefing two months ago, Superintendent Claudia sold me out to the E.B.P.B. and they in turn used this information to their advantage right after the organization promoted me. It's funny how sometimes in life when you get the very thing you'd been hoping for, you discover that the inconveniences outweigh the prospects by a ton. I looked at the bars on my shoulders as I dressed, Inspector Parker of the Elite Border Patrol Bureau.

I would give anything to be a sergeant again, to not feel the guilt about what I allowed Christopher to do to me and not live with the secret shame of wanting him to do it again. A thousand gypsy curses on the Neutral Zone. I would never have met Christopher, I wouldn't have been disgraced and I would be able to sleep at night without thinking of him, remembering the unfathomable depths of his chocolate brown eyes piercing into my soul as his fingers...

The only reason I didn't quit the force at this point in time was because, firstly, I knew the Bureau would send someone else after Christopher and his alleged operation and secondly, that whatever we found could never see Christopher MacPherson arrested. The information would just see his illegal businesses closed down, and if he was indeed guilty of the other crime, we would pass that information over to the authorities in that jurisdiction because we had no powers of arrest in the Neutral Zone.

He was accused of harboring citizens of Androfemur namely female prisoners, against their will and forcing them into labor, sometimes even prostitution. When I had first heard of the accusations, I scoffed at Christopher forcing any woman to do anything against her will. I was pretty sure they were willingly doing so.

Then they informed me that neither the prisoners nor MacPherson was authorized to have Androfemians work in the Neutral Zone but that some corrupted officials were luring more and more women into the Neutral zone with promises of new prospects. Although that was not entirely the E.B.P.B's business the defection was, as Androfemur had a treaty to honor. However, I was yet to be convinced as to why I was required to compromise my freedom, and maybe even more, for the sake of advancing this investigation.

Clearly, they realized that I believed their motives although movingly patriotic, to be a little weak. So they brought out the big guns, showing me pictures of mutilated female corpses of women who were last in the employment of the MacPherson brothers. I gagged at the picture of a woman's eye popping out of her head in the last, bloody photo. Without a doubt there was a problem. Christopher and his brother could be murderers. This was something more up my alley. If I gathered evidence that any of them were indeed guilty, I would hunt them to the ends of the earth to bring these women justice.

They wanted me to make first contact, to go to his place, but I knew Christopher. He was too intelligent not to suspect something, he was too astute to believe that I missed his corruption and I couldn't stay away. We had only been in each other's company a lifetime ago, he probably forgot my name. Besides, I clearly recall our affair being one sided. He didn't want me, he even said as much, that he would get someone else to take care of his needs.

I would have to be very convincing to ever get him to lower his defenses to lay siege to his fortresses. Particularly, I would need copious amounts of time and access in order to run through his office documents and snoop around his businesses and his apartments. It was a stroke of luck that the E.B.P.B. through their back channels, discovered that Demetri

MacPherson had been making very discreet inquiries as to when I would be in the Neutral Zone next. To what end I hadn't the foggiest, but there was my in and I intended to explore it to see where it lead.

CHAPTER 17

Christopher had very few regrets in his life. He was not a man to baulk at a chance and he certainly never spent his days examining the ashes of what could have been. Nevertheless, he found himself doing exactly that. It had been two months and seven days. He could smell her on his breath and taste her confectionary on his tongue. He was an honest to goodness living martyr. Why did he not just take her? She was offering him herself like a sacrificial virgin and he could not bring himself to use her. If he had taken her, he was sure he would have forgotten her face by now, her mesmerizing smoky eyes that haunted the passages of his mind. He was sure he would have slept undisturbed. Jane Parker's memory was a nuisance, especially when he had a desk full of work to get through in the next two hours and a meeting with two Congressmen and a reformed Mob boss before breakfast tomorrow.

Two months ago, Demetri had found him a girl that night. She bored him completely. He asked his brother for a brown-eyed mahogany-haired girl. When she came in, she didn't interest him, not even a little bit. Her coloring was off and she did not smell like Jane and after he kissed her, he realized her lips were not made of nectar. There was a turning point after that. Demetri made sure there was a new girl waiting for him every night in his office. He dismissed all of them, because they were not Jane. Last week he made it a point of asking Demetri not to send any more girls to his office.

It was 11:57 p.m. Christopher was exhausted, a wrecked man. All he wanted to do was to close his eyes but he knew he would find no peace because sleep would not come to him.

He was tormented every time he closed his eyes. He could remember her haunting eyes begging him to show her what to do to please him. He dropped into his swivel chair and cradled his head in his palms as if searching for some consolation.

It was approaching the hour that he allowed himself to replay his agony.

"Why didn't you say that before? I've been holding back." He could hear her reprimanding him.

When he remembered how she lowered his hands to her pulsating pubic area, he cried out in a strangled whisper, "Oh, Janey."

Suddenly, there was a feminine hand on his shoulder. His body went rigid. Without looking around, he viciously commanded in a flat tone, "Get out!" then belatedly added, "before I throw you out."

But the hand remained on his shoulder this time gently massaging away the tension there. Deliberately he turned around to give the trespasser a strongly worded rebuke, when…

Demetri had always been a great brother, a pain in his ass but this, this was…

The female opened her mouth to speak, but he quickly placed his forefinger on her lips. He didn't even want her to speak, else she might destroy the facsimile of perfection that was before him. This woman could have been Janey's twin, the hair, the eyes identical. He wanted to pretend that she was her tonight. He couldn't go on like this wishing and wanting her, it was ripping him apart.

He covered her lips with his own demanding, searching, stealing, drinking. He thought, *My goodness, this woman whoever she is, is first-class.* He ripped at her pantyhose, slipped her underwear to the side and fingered her. She ground against his intrusion. She was wet, hot and writhing against him. He quickly unzipped his pants and forcefully entered her. A sob slipped from her throat and a tear from her eyes, but he didn't notice. All he felt was this vixen moving in tandem with his body. She was pinned to his office walls, one leg over his thigh, her tight pussy was over his engorged cock, and he was covering her moans with his lips. When he released his assault on her lips, he ripped her blouse aside and took possession of her breast with his tongue, while still plunging upwards into her wet passage. A groan ripped from her throat followed by, "Oh, God, Christopher," she whispered into his ear, "Please, I've missed you too."

Her convulsions were quickly followed by his. It was too late, he hadn't stopped himself, like he knew he should. The profanity should have been a dead giveaway. When she told him that she missed him too, he instantly realized his mistake. Somehow Janey had come back to him and instead of taking her like she deserved to be taken, he had used her like the prostitute he thought she was. But her utterances were his undoing. He experienced an out of body phenomenon. He knew he should have stopped once he discovered his oversight but he couldn't. He stood for a long time, plastering his body against hers pinning it to the wall smelling her hair.

"Oh, Janey, oh, Janey," he sighed apologetically. He wanted to say he was sorry but the words sounded shallow in his mind. He would spend the rest of their lives making it up to her. He loved her, there was no doubt about that now. He stepped back still holding her close to him, allowing her to fall frontal on him. She turned up her tear-stained face at him and smiled.

"Honey, I am so sorry," he said anyway.

She stiffened in his arms and pulled away. "Why are you sorry, Christopher MacPherson?"

He hurt her and now she was angry. She had all rights, of course, he had used her wrongly.

"Did I not please you?" she inquired with dripping sarcasm.

Her insecurity had the effect of evoking a broad smile on his face as he realized that somehow, she failed to acknowledge that he had hurt her. Instead she was now questioning her desirability.

"Well I guess you could always find someone else to ease your pain," she put in viciously, straightening her skirts while making deliberate strides towards the door.

"You're wearing a dress." His observation halted her premature exodus.

She turned to face him. "Yes, I find them to be ever so practical now." She added this lie wiping her tear stained face with the back of her hands; the truth was she had worn it for him.

Christopher poured her a drink of scotch, walked over to her and placed it into her hands. She accepted it but she didn't lift her face to meet his. She was still hurt, hurt at the prospect of him wanting another to please him no doubt.

He returned to his office couch, sat down and studied her. It was evident she had a notion that he had many lovers and that he was somehow making a comparison of sorts. Her obvious jealousy made his groin tightened. He wanted to take her again.

"Janey, come," he coaxed softly patting one of the cushions he sat next to. She stubbornly refused to acknowledge his entreaty. "Janey? Look at me… Please," he demanded softly, and when she did, he repeated his request "Come."

This time she walked over to him with apprehension in her steps. Jane thought, *did he want to do the same thing they did just now*? Her thoughts were racing as she got closer. She didn't know what just happened, and how she felt about it. But when she was with him, she had no thoughts, just feelings, overwhelming feelings of… More.

She was suddenly seated next to him, with her eyes downcast, not because she was fearful but because she was nervous. All she could smell was him, her scent and his intermingled, his hair, his breath, his desire and she wanted more. She suspected he already knew what she was feeling which meant he had an advantage. He took her chin in his hand and tilted her head up. She looked up at his eyes, saying a silent prayer for him not to come too close. Not yet.

He read apprehension in her eyes. He wasn't sure why, since she had come to him. He smiled, laying down taking her with him. She collapsed willingly on his body. He wasn't quite sure either of them were ready to discuss the explosive feelings they were evidently both having.

Fatigue swept over him like a wave and he suddenly didn't have the energy to pretend anymore with her. "I thought you were a ghost, I've been tormented by the smell of you, the loss of you…"

She looked up and read sincerity in his eyes and it was her undoing.

"Never leave me again, Janey."

"Why?" she asked, instinctively knowing his answer.

"I haven't had a good night's rest since you left." He added knowing that if he was not straight with her, other commitments would eventually take her away, "I've wanted you in my bed every day, I've been haunted by the memory of you. Never leave me, Janey."

"Can I leave you long enough to go to the bathroom?" she joked, as he caught her in his embrace.

"No," he emphatically announced, pulling her face away from his body to plant a kiss on her lips. She laughed. God he wasn't sure he had ever seen her laugh and now his world would always be dim if she wasn't there to illuminate his day with her smile.

"I'm a mess. I'm not fit to be seen in public," she said, straightening her mussed, mahogany curls.

"I have no intention of ever sharing you with anyone, ever." He squeezed and then released her. "But I will allow you a ten-minute bathroom break. Don't make me come in after you," he warned as he smelled the perfume of her hair once more.

She closed the door falling back on it. She was finally alone. She was in new territory. None of her training could have ever prepared her for the situation she was in now.

Her plan worked. Christopher wanted her around, at least for now. That meant he would want to be with her like that again. She would be required to have sex with him again. The act itself was exciting, a bit of an adrenaline rush, but she wasn't sure how long she could continue deceiving him. She found that she wanted to open up to him when she was with him and this ran counter to her mission.

She peeled off her dress. That was another thing, dresses were so impractical, making any sort of maneuvers in them very difficult. Christopher seemed to like them so she would have to continue wearing them. She sighed now as she looked at her underwear. There was some blood in her underwear. She was told that this may happen. At least her seniors told her something. She decided to take a shower. Leaving her clothes on the towel rack, she stepped into a bath that was as big as a small pool. It seemed Christopher never did anything in half measures.

Ten minutes later, Christopher made good on his threat and joined her in the shower. "Missed me?" he said, smiling mischievously.

Christopher was a naked statue before her, beautifully sculptured, fully erected. Her awe was apparent. She swallowed her salivation.

Then she inquired innocently "Have you come in for a shower as well? Your bath is certainly big enough for twenty people."

"I've come to lend my assistance," he said, taking up the bottle of liquid soap. "Shampoo, or no shampoo?"

Janey replied "Oh, noooo, I washed my hair today."

"Well, maybe another time."

"Turn around," he demanded.

She asked, "For what?" knowing he was up to something.

"Janey, you must learn to trust me, as I only have your best interests at heart."

Jane rolled her eyes and turned around.

Christopher swept her hair up, rolled it into a bun and piled it at the top of her head very efficiently, so much so that she wondered how many times he'd done the act before. When he started to apply the soap and work his magic from the nape of her neck, down her shoulders and over the small of her back, moaning inexplicably escaped her lips. She'd never experienced anything like that before.

"Lower?" he asked.

She heard him say something but she was too far away to care. As Christopher applied soap to her derriere she jumped. She couldn't remember anyone ever touching her there.

He wanted to sink his teeth into her rump, it was so plump and delicate, but he resisted the urge. Kneeling instead, he soaped her legs back to front, then front to back, working his hand straight up to her tush at the back and her clit at the front.

He took the shower head and began to rinse, ever so slowly, slipping his finger into her pussy, inch by inch as he rinsed. She pushed back every time he inched closer. When his fingers easily inserted all the way into her slit he knew she was ready.

He then whispered, "Trust me, Janey?

She moaned. He turned her around to face him, this time peering passed her desire filled eyes into her soul and he said, "I'm going to fuck you, do you want me to?"

Jane, gagging for all of him, covering his lips with her own she indicated she was ready.

Christopher whispered, "Turn around."

Jane found she couldn't resist him. She would do anything he wanted now, with all her inaugural apprehensions out of the way she complied.

Christopher said, "Bend over and hold onto your knees, and don't let go."

She fell forward, doing as he asked.

Christopher, holding his cock, inserted it inch by inch as she pushed back incrementally. When there was no room between them, he stayed there for a while, whilst she adjusted to him. He inched out, then forward, his pubic area slamming into her scrumptious butt, the water of the shower making a slapping sound.

He asked, tentatively holding onto his sanity, "More?"

She moaned, he shouted, "You have to say it, Janey."

She blurted out impatiently, "Yes, Chris. Fuck me!"

This time with his primal urges released, he slammed into her over and over, the slapping sound of the water exciting them both, until he emptied his soul into her.

Neither of them fell asleep until after three thirty a.m.

The next morning, Demetri unlocked the office door with his personal keys and discovered his brother entwined with his lover on the office couch. He gingerly shut the door behind him, allowing his brother to get some much needed rest.

CHAPTER 18

Jane:

I awoke the next morning, skin to skin with Christopher, nothing separating us except for an errant blanket which seemed to be half covering us both whist playing hide and go seek intermingling between our naked bodies. Christopher covered me three quarter way with his hand flung possessively over my breast. My left arm was pinned between Chris and the inner part of the couch. I was trapped, my body was trapped, my mind was trapped. On a morning like this I would escape my confusion by taking an exceedingly long run. But I was barricaded.

Panic welled up inside of me. I needed to get away. I shifted up and tried to escape through the only portal I could find.

As I managed to detangle my entire body from the sheets, the couch and Christopher, I heard a muffled voice say, "Escaping?"

I froze. not sure what I was going to do now that I was caught. I wasn't sure what kind of voodoo sex was. First, I was doing everything that Chris wanted without examination, without protest, and now it was as if Chris was reading my mind. I wasn't liking this situation at all.

CHAPTER 19

Christopher:

I was awake for some time, in a daze, not thinking for the first time in a long time what the rest of my day held. Feeling warm smooth skin against my own, wrapped up in the smell of Jane. My mind free at last and at rest. Not wondering where she was and if I'd ever see her again. Being free to love her and be with her the way I needed to be.

Suddenly, she began to move beneath me. Feeling my own arousal, my body moved, needing no encouragement at all where Jane was concerned.

I laid there as a curious spectator waiting to see what she would do. Generally acknowledging her inexperience but instinctively feeling she would require little tutelage when it came to love making. All notions were dispelled when she demanded that I fuck her last night. As my mind remembered, so did my body and I was as rigid as I waited in anticipation.

I could feel her sliding her hand and a leg out from under me. Was she getting up? Trying to leave? Maybe she was going to the washroom. But why was she moving so quietly as if she didn't want to wake me? Maybe she wanted me to rest, didn't want to disturb me. Maybe she needed to leave. Janey had a job, commitments. She didn't live here. Janey and I were not free like other couples to pursue a normal relationship, time and geography were against us. Now that I had found her, I couldn't let go, not just now. So I asked, "Escaping?"

CHAPTER 20

She was escaping. She wanted to get the hell out of there, clear her mind, decide her next steps. She felt the room begin to close in on her. Her back was to him. She was putting on her clothes, She hadn't said anything because nothing would come to mind. She didn't know what she was supposed to say. Chief Debbie Pooran briefed her on copulation after checking all her vaccinations were current and that she received a six month contraception shot. She told Jane that men didn't like to cuddle or talk after sex. Jane wasn't prepared for the morning after conversation, she always planned to sneak out. Think, think, think.

Christopher wasn't sure what he could say to make her stay. Vanity and wanting made him think she wanted him and she returned to be with him. He was slowly realizing he was wrong. Questions to which he had no answers seems to invade his mind in no particular order. How long was she here for? What was she doing in the Neutral Zone? Was she on a prisoner transport run? Was she here for one night? Is this the reason for her sudden departure? Why wasn't she answering him?

So he asked, "I never asked, what brings you to the Neutral Zone?

Her hands froze as she was on her last dress button. She already had a cover story but the question still took her aback. She turned around smiled and gave him her prepared speech. "I'm on vacation."

"In the Neutral Zone?" he asked incredulously.

"It can't be that bad, you live here."

He smiled at her witty come back, "For how long?" he asked, buying himself as much time with her as he could.

"A couple months." Jane intended to keep her answers vague. It was a technique used for maneuverability, to avoid being caught in a lie. She decided to take charge of the conversation by turning the eyes of scrutiny off of herself.

"So what are your plans this morning, Chris?"

"You called me Chris."

"And?" she asked smiling, bending to slip on her shoes

"No one calls me Chris."

"There's a first time for everything I guess, but you never answered my question."

He thought, *she was leaving so why was she interested in the goings on of his day? Was she trying to make conversation or did she want something? Regardless of her charming conversation, her body language indicated to him that all she wanted to do was to get away unobstructed.*

He played along. "I have some meetings, nothing I couldn't cancel."

There. He answered and left an opening for her.

CHAPTER 21

Jane:

What was Christopher playing at. Was he offering to escort me around the Neutral Zone? It was obvious he wanted something but I wasn't sure what he wanted. So I said, "I feel like you want me to say something, but I'm not sure what it is Chris."

He smiled and said, "I want you to stay."

Becoming less and less convinced of my get away plans, I replied, "I can't, I have to get currency and check into my hotel room."

I walked over to the couch and joined him again, this time fully clothed and explained my concern. "I may lose my reservation, I never checked in last night,"

Christopher inquired, "Which hotel?"

"Why?"

"Janey, you ask too many questions."

I sprang up from the couch, walking strides for the door this time, angry at his overbearing attitude. Did women accept men speaking to them like that in the Neutral Zone? It wasn't something I would ever accept or get accustomed to.

"Where are you going?" he sprang up too, grabbing my forearm. Reading my expression he asked, "What's wrong?"

I was curious by nature. My investigation required me to ask questions. This wasn't going to work. So I blurted out in irritation, "Christopher, I'm not sure how it's done here, but I'm not a doll. I have a mind, thoughts of my own, plans of my own. You expect me not to ask you questions while you make plans for me, but I always will. If that's not cool with you then let's say our goodbyes."

Almost as soon as I said it, I regretted it. I knew if he said goodbye I would be in trouble. He was my access key into the investigation I was assigned to conduct.

CHAPTER 22

Christopher:
What the fuck. Within three minutes flat, I'm falling in love with her, planning our future, and now she's giving me ultimatums and walking out of my life forever?

I remembered the words of Sister Agatha. Apologize even if you don't mean it. "I'm sorry, what do you need, Jane?"

I tried to read her expression, desperately wanting to know what she wanted. If I could only get to that truth, then I could get what I wanted. Which was Jane.

CHAPTER 23

Jane:

The question took me aback. *What did I need?*

One moment, I wanted to escape Chris' office, the next he apologised to me and I wanted to be in his arms. I'd never been so confused in my life. If this was the after effects of sex, I hated it! Ever since our first encounter, I wanted nothing but his lips on me, him inside me, on top of me, placing his hand on the small of my back. I couldn't think straight, let alone know what I needed. Unexpectedly, my stomach lurched audibly, interrupting the moment and gave me an out, "Apparently, I need breakfast," I announced, giving him a mischievous grin.

CHAPTER 24

So, he ordered up a breakfast buffet from his kitchen restaurant and she ate breakfast. Two poached eggs, three pancakes, two sausages, three strips of bacon, one mug of coffee. She ate in silence, she watched him as he watched her in silence. He patiently looked on at the mystery that was Jane Parker. She in full command of her faculties now that she was fed. She knew what she must do.

"You're not eating?" she asked.

"No," he answered simply.

"May I pour you some tea or coffee?"

"No," he replied

"Can't I interest you in anything?" she asked playfully, leaving her dishes then settling as daintily as she possibly could next to him.

"You know what I want Jane. Why are you playing games?" he asked quietly.

She realized he was in earnest and somehow he lost the playful mood he was in last night. Was he really offended when she told him she had her own mind? They didn't know each other at all but she wasn't liking his current mood. His quiet impatience, his guarded look wasn't something she was sure she could deal with. Undercover work was hard. She couldn't go on pretending, not with him. Most of her cover had to be true, she would only lie when she absolutely had to. She had to at least be herself with him. She hated fakes and it was proving impossible to be one.

She answered him honestly for the first time since they awoke. "Chris, I don't know who I'm supposed to be with you. I feel like you want me to be something I'm not"

"Why would you say that?"

"I wanted to go take a run this morning, to clear my head," she said

"Who's stopping you, Jane?"

"You. You got up and started to question me about what I was doing, where I was going. I'm not accustomed to that," she explained.

"You're not accustomed to people asking you about your whereabouts?"

"No. I live alone." She stood up and shook her head. "I'm confused. I feel like I'm doing everything wrong."

He said, "Jane, sit!" then he tempered his demand by saying, "sorry, please have a seat." As she sat, he drew closer. "I'm figuring this out too, I should be in a meeting now, but instead I'm here."

"Why?"

"Well, put simply, I wanted to be in your company."

"Why?" she asked again

"We had such a wonderful night. I was hoping for a wonderful morning as well, maybe even a wonderful day with you."

"Don't you have other important things to do?"

"Well, I guess I have. But nothing as important as being here with you, watching you eat."

"You're weird," she said smilingly.

He thought, *no I'm in love with a woman who is not in love with me, but I'll be patient.*

He was guessing this was her first relationship, first affair. She was a virgin, so last night was her first time. She was almost thirty but still an innocent in the ways of love. She was also stubborn, opinionated and mistrustful of him, he realized. She, no doubt knew a thing or two about his business dealings. How could a woman like her ever want to be with a man like him? He would have to do something drastic, something he'd never done with any other woman in his life, he would open up to her. He would convince Janey that she could trust him. He would show her everything was alright. Although they didn't know each other, he could sense she had a big heart and he was willing to do what he must to capture it.

So he said, getting off the couch, "You're right, of course." Heading for the door, he said, " I'll have Francisco, take you to your hotel now. Bye, Jane."

To which she replied, "Bye," to a closed door.

One moment he was saying he wanted to spend the day with her, the next moment he was walking out on her. Chris' whiplash decisions were not something Jane was sure she could put up with for the next four months.

Approximately twenty minutes later, Francisco came to the door, knocked lightly and entered. He lifted an eyebrow of inquiry but actually said nothing to her until they were both seated in Chris' limo. He asked, "Where to?"

Hotel Infinito was mediocre and unremarkable as hotels go. It was one large sixteen-storey semi-circular building with an outdoor pool. It was exactly the type of place a public servant could afford, thus the choice was made by the E.B.P.B.

Trouble was, a building like this would have been torn down in Androfemur. For starters it was not eco-friendly. In Androfemur, all electricity was generated from solar energy. Although Jane only had a modest house herself which was sparsely furnished, it was beautifully designed, built using ecofriendly materials and located across the way from a huge forested area. This hotel was situated in the heart of the metropolis with no greenery in sight. Jane Parker was spoilt by fresh air and beautiful freshwater ponds.

As Jane checked in, the girl at the front desk unexpectedly upgraded her to the Presidential suite. At least she would stay in a bigger room.

CHAPTER 25

A week passed. Christopher didn't reach out. Jane knew that he knew where she was staying, that much was obvious when he asked Francisco to convey her to her hotel. On the second day, when she enquired about the billing, she found out she wasn't upgraded by the hotel but that Christopher's credit covered her entire bill and for her upgrade.

Yet, he wasn't reaching out. No flowers, no notes, no phone calls. What was she expecting? Day four she began to examine why he may not have come around and the answer was obvious. She wanted her freedom, she told him as much and he let her have it. She concluded that having a heterosexual relationship was very tricky. The E.B.P.B. taught her the male ego was very fragile, but this was ridiculous. He refused to call because he couldn't control her? Or maybe he had somebody else all the while he was saying that he missed her. Maybe it wasn't realistic to expect a man like Christopher to care about what a nobody like Jane wanted.

Jane was coming back from a long run when she realized it had been a week and Christopher hadn't reached out. She concluded that she would have to go to the mountain, since it was clear the mountain was not coming to her. She wanted intel from him, she was investigating him. She had more at stake than he did and she would do her job as she always did.

If he wasn't coming to her, she would find him.

CHAPTER 26

As Jane stepped into one of Christopher's clubs, Turner Club, all eyes were on her. The women of Androfemur always said that the correct dress would cut a whopping job down to size. She never really understood that saying until now. Dressed in a fitted, blood-red dress. One shoulder bare and a mid-thigh slit which revealed her leg with every advance. Her hair styled down, falling about her mid back, she made her way to a private enclave, willing Chris to come to her now before her courage failed her.

Someone did come, but it most definitely was not Chris.

"Excuse me, ma'am," a paunchy male who approached her table slurred.

Jane looked up and smiled, trying to be polite.

He continued, "Was wondering, how much it would cost me, for you to show me and my friends a good time?" He looked over his shoulder to some other men, supposedly his friends.

She returned to looking at the menu and ignored him, hoping he would get the hint and leave.

Chapter 27

Christopher:

I was about to leave my office, to go to Jane's hotel. My plan was, I would turn up at her room with flowers, apologize for not reaching out. I reasoned I'd given her more than enough time and space to make up her mind as to if she wanted me as much as I wanted her. Unwittingly, I caught a flash across the monitors located in my office where I observed a blur of red sail across the screen. The woman wearing the dress was familiar.

Out of all the joints in the Neutral Zone, she had to walk in here looking like that. My patrons were the upper crust of the Neutral Zone but they were accustomed to getting what they wanted and an unaccompanied female, dressed to draw attention to herself was invitation enough.

Chapter 28

Jane:

She spoke through bared teeth, "I said, I'm waiting on someone."

"Well, darling, I ain't see nobody here but you and I. Are you sure he's coming?"

I was determined to smash his head in with the wine bottle my hand was currently clasp unto. I had purposely asked the waiter to leave the bottle in case a weapon was required, especially as I wasn't sure Chris was coming. For all I knew he left before my arrival.

The plan was an expensive one. The dress, the entire bottle of wine and still no Chris.

" You know what I think?" his pestering continued

"Actually, I don't care," I replied, gripping the bottle's neck even harder, ready to swing at a moment's notice.

Chapter 29

"Do we have a guest?" she heard a familiar male voice ask.

The drunkard smartened up, apologized quickly, then vanished. There he was, handsome as ever in beaver brown alligator skin shoes, a navy-blue suit, crisps white shirt, gold cufflinks and a displeased look, if ever she saw one.

"Get up!" was all he said before he grabbed her arm, yanking her out of her seat.

By now several onlookers were amused and outright gaping at their tête-à-tête. Straightened up, she snatched herself from his grip and walked out on her own, determined to get her car and go back to her hotel room.

She burst through the exit doors and handed her chit to the valet, who after supposedly seeing his angry boss, decided to disappear.

Jane said nothing. Christopher said nothing until a limo pulled up in front of them both. He demanded, "Get in!"

She challenged him with fire in her eyes, "Or what?"

It took him one step to reach her ear, into which he whispered, "You wind me up."

Damn him. She was angry at him. She wanted to remain angry, so she was not expecting his honesty. She grinned at him and said playfully, "No, it's you who make me crazy, Chris."

He held her free hand. "I see a problem. What do we do now?"

She turned to him and said, "I guess we could make each other crazy somewhere else."

His heart leapt but he kept a straight face. "Do you have a suggestion as to where we may go, my lady?"

Then she said the thing she knew he wanted to hear. "I trust you. You choose."

CHAPTER 30

As they entered the car, they were all over each other hungrily kissing exposed and unexposed flesh. The last thing Christopher had the cognizance to do was to send the partition up between them and Francisco.

Christopher slid Jane's dress off her shoulder, pulling down the top part to her waist. He hitched up the rest of her dress, upward and over her hip, whilst she loosened his tie, ripping what looked like a brand-new shirt, buttons cascading to the ground. He in turn dragged her underwear off, balled it up and gave it a good whiff. She laughed at his caveman tactics.

Like two long lost atoms they merged. She cried out his name. His outpour of affection was a groan. Just like that they were one again, holding each other like on the first night, until the limo came to a stop.

Jane's eyes popped open with apprehension, half expecting Francisco to open the door on their love making.

He smiled lazily and said, "Don't worry, all my staff are discrete. Besides he's gone now."

She smiled sheepishly and laughed. "Where are we Chris?"

"We're home"

CHAPTER 31

Jane:

My eyes opened and adjusted to the room. The colours were surprising, an array of greens — lime green, olive green, shamrock green and emerald green mainly emerald green and creams. The bed was centered, the linens tasteful silks, a full length mirror on one of the doors, most likely the entrance to the walk in closets. There was an aesthetically pleasing gold vanity, with a green poof loveseat and matching golden legs. Chris had again proven himself to be a man of discriminating taste. There was one thing missing though. Where was Chris?

She found one of his shirts in his closet and left the room in search of him. When she found him, he was on the phone.

"I don't care what you need to get it done, just get it done today."

She interrupted him by sneaking up on him, but he turned as she got closer and he almost knocked her over with the force of his rotation.

Tripping each other up, they both landed on the rug.

She laughed and said in good humour, "Good morning."

He responded by kissing her deeply, "Now, it is a very good morning."

"Imagine, I got up this morning and thought you were kidnapped"

"Did you miss me?"

"For one whole minute it was a mad panic," she teased rolling her eyes.

"Honestly, if I knew I would be missed so much by you I would've never left."

Jane asked him first this time, "What are you doing this morning?"

"Hmm, are we sharing?" he teased. Jane laughed, remembering the morning he asked her what her plans were.

She asked, cocking her head to one side, "Is this going to be a revenge thing?"

"No, not at all. I had to make an urgent call and truth be told, I didn't want to spook you. I want you in my bed for a long time," he replied.

Damn, his heartfelt responses caught her off guard every time. She replied, "It would be my pleasure to make that happen, just as long as you're in bed with me."

He stood up, pulling her up after him. "I'm afraid I have to disappoint you this morning."

Her response was a lifted eyebrow.

"I have one particular meeting I cannot get out of and the site visit of a new building I purchased recently."

"So what do I do all day?"

"It's a big house. You can explore the house, or the stables in my absence."

"Is there any place off limits?"

"From you?" He kissed her forehead "No. Got to run. Ask Deidra for breakfast, and Francisco will take you anywhere you want to go today."

As Jane slowly took the stairs, she watched him hop into his car and disappear down the long elegant driveway. She was finally alone, with the house to herself. She would investigate unobstructed. She got breakfast then announced, in a most emphatic tone, that she was going to explore the house. Deidra, who barely spoke English, either didn't understand her at all, or didn't care.

With her trusty X-Ray vision attachment, she searched all ten en suite bedrooms, dining room, gaming room and finally Chris' study, eventually prizing open a locked draw which looked promising. She was examining the last of the contents of Chris' office draw when the door creaked opened. She snatched the attachment from the side of her face in time to look up at the intruder. There was Francisco with that blasé expression he always wore scrutinizing her intently.

Already prepared with an excuse, Jane explained that she didn't have Chris' number and that she was looking for writing material and paper to leave Chris a note as she was heading out herself.

She left Francisco standing in the library, with a prewritten hand note under a paper weight. After that, she called a cab, which came in record time, and departed from the house for Turner Club, where she had left her rental. She didn't need Francisco reporting her every movement to Chris. She knew he was loyal but it was really creepy the way he snuck up on a person.

After Turner Club, she checked in with her handler and reported to her that she searched Chris' house and there was nothing to be found there.

She retired to her hotel, to find the usual day receptionist gone and her suite filled with flowers a note and a key. No doubt they were from Chris. What was he up to?

CHAPTER 32

Jane was in her pajamas when there was a knock at her hotel room door. She didn't order room service. The maid made the bed before she arrived. She wasn't expecting anyone. She found her black, chromed Glock pistol, cocked it and answered the door with the chain on.

Chris was on the other side with more flowers. She pulled back the chain, opened the door and walked back to her safe where she kept her gun, locking the weapon inside with a special code.

"What a welcome, gun in hand? It's good to see you to," he said incredulously.

"I'm sorry, Chris." She walked up to him, planted a kiss on him and said, "It's the Neutral Zone. Anyone could have been at my door."

He closed the door behind him realizing he had an opening here. "This is why I took you home last night. I thought you would be comfortable at my place."

"I was, I am." She stopped.

"But what?" he added knowing there was something she was not saying.

She tried honesty. "In the spirit of full disclosure, I would feel a lot better knowing my every move wasn't being reported to you by Francisco. That is why I left."

"My place is heavily guarded and completely secured. Francisco wasn't there for security, I left him there to take you where you wanted to go," he chided her. "I saw your rental. It's not exactly safe, its hackable, unarmored and not connected to emergency response servers."

Jane smiled, "Are you calling my car a piece of junk?"

Christopher hugged her from behind, girding his arms around her waist. "Yes, and I'm allowed to worry about you, am I not?"

Although she felt some comfort in his embrace, she turned around, squinting at him. "I don't know. Do you want to be?"

"If I wasn't clear just now, I'm officially asking you to be my lady." He smiled at the thought. "What do you say?"

Jane pretended to think about it for a while and then asked him, "What would that entail? That sounds like a very difficult job... being your lady."

"Oh, it's very hard," he said pressing his rigid shaft against her abdominal area.

"Oh, well, I suppose I can do hard."

He tasted her tongue. She teased, kissing him along the neck, down the chest area opening one button at a time until, she was at his trousers which were bursting at the seams. She loosened his belt buckle, pulling the entire belt out of the loops with one swoop.

He turned her around, she turned back to face him and cautioned him, "Patience."

She continued to strip him of his underwear, until his manhood was fully engorged and in front of her like a delicious meal, pulsing and ready to be swallowed. And swallow him she did.

He lost his mind, motioning her head to go deeper, Jane, keeping the rhythm steady until he emptied himself into her mouth. She was not unpleasantly surprised to feel the heat and the salt of the liquid at the back of her throat. She swallowed one last time, stood up and smiled.

Christopher's legs trembled at the intensity of his ejaculation. She guided him to her bed and joked, "I guess the job is mine."

He snorted a laugh, unable to do nothing much else.

It wasn't like the time in the shower. They made love this time, slowly, he giving everything and she taking her pleasure at all angles. When they were spent, they laid spooning in each other's arms.

Chris whispered into her hair. "Great job, baby."

CHAPTER 33

Jane was having a most glorious dream for which she never wanted to wake from. Christopher's cock was pressed up hard against her ass. She in turn was gyrating against his manhood. The pleasure was so palpable she could feel herself salivating.

Then his mouth was nibbling and kissing her bottom. He turned her over, kissing her cunt, licking and sucking. Taking her clitoris into his mouth, then manipulating it back and forth. Her nipples strained as his hand squeezed her breast over and over. It was only as she was cumming, that her eyes flung opened and she realized it wasn't a dream.

When she returned to earth, Chris whispered, "Morning, beautiful."

She replied, "Chris, is this your ploy so that I would never leave your bed?"

He unashamedly replied, "Yes."

She said sleepy, "Good. It's working," rubbing her tush against his cock, signaling she wanted more. He lifted her leg inserting himself into her and hugging her from behind. He began to awaken her already heightened senses.

She moaned as he plunged deeper. She held onto her pillow, turning over to give him the full view of her derriere. As he pounded, she screamed, "Fuck me, fuck me Chris," into her pillow as he held unto her head. He plunged deeper and deeper until he lost control and emptied himself into her. Both of them collapsed into her sheets, giggling like two teenagers.

"It's official, Janey," he announced.

"What is?" she asked.

"You've ruined me for everyone else." He smiled, returning to their spooning position. He had a full day ahead which he was ready to cancel. There was no way he was leaving her bed again today.

CHAPTER 34

Jane awoke, breakfast was ordered and in hot plates, and Chris was gone again. There was a note though, stuck on the pillow he slept on. It read "*Check out bay #1 in the basement, you will need the key, Love Chris.*

Chris wasn't pulling any punches. He continually showed her nothing other than he wanted to be with her. Jane's heart soared at the thought of his devotion. Her clitoris throbbed as she remembered his mouth on and in her.

Her romantic reverie was interrupted as she remembered her true purpose for being in the Neutral Zone. She groaned into her pillow, this time not with pleasure but disgust. She hated her job. She never thought she would think about her job that way, but she felt nothing but revulsion at the thought of her having to continue to deceive Chris. She snatched the key from the flowers and headed to the basement via the elevator still disgusted with what she had to do.

Bay #1 was located in the employee's parking lot. She also observed that this was the only area with cameras trained on them. In Bay # 1 was parked the most beautiful man-made creation. If the new Z Mercedes series made a baby with the Classic Range Rover, their baby would look like this. Trouble was Bay # 1 was reserved for the manager. This Jane knew because when she first arrived, she scouted this area out as a possible means of escape.

Walking back to the elevator, she went up to the front desk and inquired as to the make and model of car driven by the manager. The new receptionist, although willing to help, was unwilling to disclose this information as the hotel was only recently brought by someone else and under new management and she was very loyal to the new boss.

Jane couldn't argue with that logic. She returned to the basement and used the remote access button on the key to unlock and start the vehicle. The hybrid answered by coming to life. So, this was Chris' surprise.

Obviously, it was too much and Jane couldn't possibly accept it, but she wanted to see the interior so badly. She forgot it was a bribe and entered the vehicle.

She would stand corrected. The outside wasn't beautiful at all, not compared to the interior, which was a work of art Michael Angelo couldn't conceive. Her hands followed the vanilla coloured interior, fitted with buttery leather seats and a console fit for a N.A.S.A. rocket launcher until she stumbled upon an envelope addressed to her. She ripped it open, more pleased at the contents of the letter than the vehicle itself, which she knew she couldn't keep under any circumstance.

It read *My Janey, since the day I met you, I couldn't get you out of my blood, you are my happiness. I had a feeling you wouldn't accept the car as a present but I want you to think of it as a wedding gift from a man to his wife. Will you marry me?*

CHAPTER 35

Christopher was missing in action for the second time that week. Demetri was left to straighten out business with the crew laying the foundation of a new club they were building. But it wasn't only that Christopher was distracted. Demetri had known his brother for over thirty years and he'd never known him to be anything else than prepared and punctual. He looked at his watch again and saw no missed calls. He knew if he tried to call his brother this early, the call would go unanswered. But Christopher was not a complete asswipe. If Demetri texted him 911, he would call him immediately. He was tempted to use their distress signal but it wasn't a genuine emergency and he didn't want to raise his brother's ire before lunch.

Demetri hopped on his antique Ducati motorbike and sped back to the office once more. He allowed his mind to wonder on his ride back. If he was being truthful with himself he would admit that he was more than just a bit concerned for his brother's well-being. He knew his brother hadn't been sleeping, that it was only three weeks ago that he walked in on Christopher with female company.

After that day, he thought everything was gravy. However, after that day he hadn't seen much of Christopher at all. He kept on disappearing without explanation which wasn't like him at all. At least CC, his Computerized Calendar would be able to say where he would be. When Demetri got back to the office, he would find out where his brother had been for the last two weeks.

Imagine Demetri's surprise when he used his key to get into the office at the Wrestlers Club to find Christopher reclined in his favourite chair, staring out the window. He was lost in thought so much so that he hadn't acknowledged someone else had entered the room.

As Demetri inched closer, his brother suddenly jerked out of his musings.

"Hey," said Christopher, inattentively, by way of a greeting.

"Hey? That all you have to say. Hey? Where have you been? You were expected at the groundbreaking for the new club!" Demetri a master at reading his brother's moods, couldn't decipher what was going on with his brother.

Whilst still in his confused state, he heard Christopher say softly under his breath to no one in particular. "What if she says no?"

Demetri having no knowledge of a third party, especially a female third party, asked, "Who is she?"

Christopher turned to his brother ,for the first time really seeing him, and said, "Janey."

Christopher immediately stood up and was headed for the door when his brother caught up to him and demanded, "Nuh uh, bro. We are finishing this conversation, Now!"

"OK, what do you want to know?" Christopher asked exasperated now that he was on the receiving end of what seemed to be an interrogation.

"For starters, who is Janey?"

"Jane Parker," Christopher said her last name as well, by way of explanation.

"Officer Jane Parker?" Demetri shouted with an incredulous grin, which was followed by, "Damn, bro."

After a moment of silence between them both, Demetri taking in the fact that his brother was dating the cop chick, Christopher adjusting to the fact he just spoke to his little brother about his love life.

Getting back to the conversation Demetri then asked, "So what do you think she's going to say no, too?"

Christopher hesitated. Demetri was his brother, he loved him but they'd never spoken about the women in their lives before. However, he rationalized that if Jane said yes , then she and Demetri would eventually meet, so there was no reason why he shouldn't know about her.

"I asked her to marry me, Demetri."

"Wow, bro, Wow!" Demetri took a breath and asked, "What do we know about this girl?"

"She's not a girl," Christopher said, with a twinkle in his eye. He continued, "And thanks to you, we know everything."

"Did you ask the investigative firm to do a background check?"

"Done, since the day after she followed you here."

"Are you saying this is my fault?" inquired Demetri, defensively.

Christopher closed the gap between himself and his brother and said sincerely, "No, I'm saying thank you, D."

Demetri's smile widened. Christopher hadn't called him that pet name since they were kids. Whoever this chic was, he liked her already. He was liking the new Christopher, or rather the old Christopher, the super big bro, who shared everything with him. This new life brought with it a constant stream of cars, businesses, clubs and restaurants, and unfortunately a lot of quarrels and friction between them.

When Christopher headed for the door this time Demetri asked over his shoulder, "When is she coming over for dinner?"

CHAPTER 36

When Jane got back to her hotel room, the down stairs receptionist placed a call to her room, telling her there was a message at the front desk and asking if it was OK for the porter to have it brought up? She said yes, and the porter was at her door before she could find her robe and put it on.

She opened the door and a young man she hadn't seen since she was at the hotel, came to the door with a waiter and an envelope on a platter, which he lowered allowing Jane to take the envelope.

She was about to tip him as she usually did the other hotel service staff, when the porter said, "Oh, no, Miss, we were specifically told not to receive any gratuities from you."

In time she would discover that their new boss, her soon to be husband, gave that edict but for now she was too excited at the letter. Excited and terrified. Was it a message from her lover or from the E.B.P.B.? Her bosses sometimes communicated in low tech code via newspaper clippings when their officers were undercover.

She opened the envelope immediately, dreading what she may find. Instead there was an embroidered letter, with gold trimming and gold writing, which began, Dear Ms Parker, and was signed, Demetri MacPherson.

After reading a very formal invitation to dinner, Jane became confused. Why did people use so much writing paper here? Why was Demetri writing to her, inviting her to an address, Christopher's home, an address she had already been to? If they both wanted her over to dinner, why wasn't Christopher inviting her over to the house? Something wasn't right.

She read the invitation again. The dress code was casual, so she didn't need a new dress but, more importantly, she wondered if it as a trap. Did Francisco blab to him and, he being the officer in the family, did he begin to suspect her motives? If he did, did he discuss his suspicions with Christopher? Was her cover blown? Should she tote her back up piece which fit snugly into her purse? She concluded that the chicken scratches below, which passed for a signature scribbled across the bottom half of the page, seem to belong to Demetri — since no two people could have such an identically illegible handwriting — she decided that she would be armed for this meeting. She was after all investigating the murder of Androfemians, and she could be the next one. Besides, one could never be too careful.

So, later that day, dressed in a pair of black fitted jeans, a maroon woolen shawl and tan high boots, she arrived at the MacPhersons' residence, driving Chris' engagement present. She contemplated taking a taxi but she decided against it in the end. If it was a trap, she would need to get out of there quickly. Besides the temptation to drive the beast of a car was too great.

Whilst passing through the security gates, Jane counted ten guards and twenty-eight cameras as she took the road leading to the main house. She had to admit, there was a lot more to see now that she was looking. She recalled the time she'd been here before. When she left via taxi it was all from a different perspective and when she came she was very occupied and hadn't noticed much of anything with her head buried in Chris' chest.

Shit, Christopher! Was he there? What did he know? Was he angry? Jane must admit, him hating her was the worst possible outcome of all of this. Her only consolation was that he would know the worst and, although he may never speak to her again, she wouldn't have to continue lying to him.

She was surprised to find that whilst she was with him, she didn't feel like she was being duplicitous. Their relationship was real to her. However, another voice in her head asked, *Is it real though?* The cold of reality hit her really hard as she realized that she would've never come looking for Christopher if it wasn't for her assignment and so their relationship, even though her feelings for him were very real, was based on a lie.

She sat in the car, gulping deep breaths, trying to fight back the tears stinging her eyes; that were promising a torrential downpour. Then there was a knock on the car door window. She looked outside her window, there was Demetri. He was alone. Well, she thought at least Chris wouldn't be there for the showdown. She would be spared the embarrassment of facing him. She quickly dabbed her eyes and lowered the beast's window.

"Was wondering if you were ever going to come out?"

"I was considering my options?"

"Jane Parker, get out that car, come give your brother in law a hug," he encouraged.

Jane, completely forgetting any possible threat and her purse with her pistol, got out of the car lost in thought.

She hesitated long enough, for him to notice something was amiss. Then he added, "You did say yes, right?"

"Not as yet, but I guess you're the first to know." she said

"I knew I liked you the first time we met. Welcome to the family, doll," he shouted gleefully embracing her and crushing her in his arms at the same time.

Later, as she sat at the kitchen counter whilst Demetri put the finishing touches on his "famous" spaghetti and meatballs dish, Jane considered what she got herself into.

Demetri said something and the words just came out. It was as if she had no control. The words weren't disingenuous they came from the heart of Jane the woman, who was in love with Christopher. And in a perfect world, they would be together. But she was Inspector Jane Parker and he was a man she was investigating for murder. What was she thinking?

She wanted to blame Demetri's infectious attitude on her slip but she couldn't fault him in this. He'd invited her to dinner it seems, to get to know her better, to tell her a bit about her brother, things he was guessing she may want answers to, seeing they hadn't known each other very long. It also seems he wanted to assure her that she was good for his brother because he kept on saying, "You're good for him, doll."

From his infectious laughter, one could clearly see he was the easy going brother. The charming one, although she would never have concluded that from their first encounter.

After the two glasses of wine she had whilst waiting on the food, Jane imagined that Demetri was a great brother and was glad to know that Chris had someone who had his back. Jane thought it must be nice to have a protective brother around. She had no siblings and always wondered what it would be like to have a sister to play with.

Suddenly, a door, maybe the front entrance, was shut loudly with much deliberation. The noise alerted them both that they were no longer alone.

They both looked up, waiting for the individual to show his or her face, when Christopher appeared.

Christopher simply said, "This looks cozy. Demetri, a word."

Demetri said to Jane with a smile, "Don't let the sauce burn, keep stirring. It's the last to go on. We won't be long."

Jane got up and went to the stove. Both brothers disappeared from sight and earshot, yet when they both spoke in the corridors there were angry whispers.

"What the fuck, Demetri, why is Jane here?"

"When you ask a girl to marry you, usually her being at your house isn't an issue, bro."

"Don't fuck with me, little brother. I let you in and you begin to meddle."

"I'm not meddling. I'm securing the deal, bro."

"She hasn't said yes, Demetri. She hasn't said yes" Christopher said a bit defensive, meandering down in a defeated tone. "You don't know her like I do. She's skittish. Now you invite her over for dinner? It's too much, I swear if you..." he stopped short at threatening his brother and the finger he was using to make his point fell at his side.

Demetri, enjoying his brother's new found insecurity, was also humbled by the power a woman can have over a man in love, even a man like Christopher. Christopher was a rock, his rock. He was never unshaken or unsure about anything or anyone and yet he was here, in his own house no less, doubting himself.

Demetri decided to put him out of his misery a bit as he began to walk back in the direction of the kitchen. "Brother, you must have a little more faith in people. It's what I keep telling you."

"Hey, what did she say?" Christopher demanded, calling him back.

"Is all good, bro. I have to get back to the sauce. Dinner is ready, come eat now."

Jane had never sat at a table that was so awkward. At first Demetri tried to lighten the air by making small talk, but Christopher kept on giving him a cold hard stare that could curdle milk. Jane, who had no idea what was going on, was attentive regardless but kept her peace. Eventually even Demetri gave up and the desert he had been hinting at earlier, a triple layer chocolate cake that was to die for, was never offered.

Jane offered to clear away the dishes. Both men shouted, "No" in unison for the same reason. Demetri knew the lovers needed to talk. Christopher asked an important question that he hadn't gotten an answer to. If she was a mob boss or a business acquaintance, he would never tolerate this delay, she would be out of business by tomorrow. Demetri figured he got them together and now he must get out of the way. Christopher was already of the opinion that Demetri had overplayed his hand and he wanted him gone to have some alone time with Jane.

Almost at once, Demetri disappeared from sight leaving Jane and Christopher seated at the table.

After a few more minutes of silence, both parties sizing each other up like rivals, Christopher asked, "More wine?" she politely declined.

This unaccustomed muteness necessitated a preemptive strike to break the tension between them in the room, so he suggested, "How about a walk?"

She jumped at the chance to leave the table where a potentially great evening all went wrong. She reasoned maybe their luck may change at another venue. As she said, "Yes," he was at her side instantly, eventually escorting her outside unto the grounds headed toward the stables.

Jane hadn't really seen the horses, nor did she search the stables the last time she was here. She calculated previously that unless there was an office at the stables then there would be nothing of mention to find there. Her limited time was better spent searching the house where potentially damning evidence was bound to be kept in a locked draw or a safe. She suddenly blushed at how the mind was such a treacherous thing. Here she was, going to make the most important discussion of Christopher's life and maybe hers too and she was thinking about work. Work which was meant only for his destruction.

Christopher noticed her change in colour and assuming she was cold, took his jacket off and wrapped it around her shoulders. Little did he know of the solitary battle that was raging within his lover. It was a war between duty and freedom, between loyalty to the truth and loyalty to one's heart, a war between saving the lives of her fellow citizens and saving her own, a war between two brave warriors, the warrior of justice and the defender of her heart. Until Christopher, Jane never thought she'd feel this way about anyone. She never thought she would abandon sound reasoning for the freedom to be herself in a way she felt she could only be with him.

As they entered the stables, Jane began to feel an emotion. Maybe it was shame. She felt unbearable guilt that she was

131

repaying his kindness for treachery which lead to her announcing, "Chris, I have something to tell you?"

She would confess everything. She loved him too much to lead him on. He deserved happiness and she, well she wasn't free to give it to him.

Christopher who, was now stroking a grey Danish warmblood said, "Janey it's OK. I've decided that whatever your answer is, we will remain friends."

Jane Parker, who knew that Christopher had only one question on his mind and that his only thought all day since he asked the question was what the possible answer might be, smiled at his bravery. She had heard that men were supposed to be brave but she had to admit the position he took was downright gallant. There was no one she admired and loved so much as him in this moment. Her heart was swollen with pride that this man loved her, chose her and wanted to be with her for the rest of their lives.

She closed the distance between them and held his free hand with hers. She then asked, "What happens if I want to be more than friends?"

His noncommittal attitude immediately turned to optimistic precaution. "Don't play with me, Janey. Are you saying what I think you're saying?"

"Yes, I'm saying yes, Chris," she replied gleefully.

He swept her up into his arms and they held each other as two drowning victims clinging to a life raft of hope. Victory would go to the defender of her heart. Tonight both warriors would rest easy until the impending battle.

CHAPTER 37

Jane:

I guess it was a stroke of luck that Christopher wanted me to be everywhere he was going now. I made a play at reading his documents in front of him; this liberty he granted me gave me unrestricted access to examine documents even in his presence. He thought that I was bored and that I wanted to help him until the wedding, but I knew better. I was searching for the evidence I was sent to collect. Since there was nothing restricting my access, I soon confirmed his claims that he was indeed smuggling in girls meant for prison, to work for him. When I questioned the women, it was as I suspected. They all seemed to want to be in his employ. They confirmed how they got their jobs, about the superior treatment they were receiving and about the payments they would receive at the end of their arrangements. I couldn't help but admire Christopher's philanthropic attitude towards these girls.

I was yet to come across anyone who had been forced into prostitution. I was yet to discover any sort of prostitution taking place. Certainly, rumors of anyone being murdered while in the employment of the MacPherson brothers proved to be none existent. But it was early days yet and my wits were still keen and focused on the investigation.

CHAPTER 38

That cop bitch was snooping about asking questions. When he told the boss, all he said was that the soon to be Mrs MacPherson had all rights to satisfy her cop curiosity. Christopher MacPherson was smitten by her, everyone could see that, but that bitch was up to something and as soon as he found out what it was, Christopher would be indebted to him.

MacPherson would see all them bitches were the same, teasing, manipulating men to get their own way.

He would show him.

That bitch was hiding something and stirring up trouble even she couldn't handle.

CHAPTER 39

Jane:

The E.B.P.B. were pressing me to get something on the MacPherson brothers. I told them there was simply nothing I could do, and I couldn't possibly fabricate evidence I didn't have. Besides, Christopher having the prisoners illegally at his club, there was nothing else to report. There were no rumors or accusations of ill treatment of the women. On the contrary, the women enjoyed it so much many of them wanted to return and work for the brothers through legal channels. Week after week it was all that I reported along with any possible associations he may have had with the more upstanding citizens of the Neutral Zone, which was of public knowledge to any who read the Neutral Zone Gazette.

After my visit to the Androfemian Outpost, I was returning to the Wrestlers club driven by Francisco. I must have fallen asleep, because one moment I was sitting in the back seat of the Limo, then I awoke in a damp place, seated in and tied to a chair with a light shining directly into my eyes. The rest of the room was dank and my dress was ripped off to the side, slinging over my shoulder down to my waist like a limp, flimsy, dead thing.

"What is your name?" the voice asked. I noted instantly it was not a normal voice. It was electrically cloaked, no doubt to hide the identity of my tormenter

"What's your name?" I asked with a bravery I didn't feel.

"You want to play games, Jane Parker; I have lots of tricks in my box over here,"

I looked over to see if I could make out a table, however I could see nothing but my own ripped dress at the waist and the tips of my tormentor's shiny dark brown shoes.

"You don't seem to be curious as to why you are here. Interesting." he commented

"I assumed you were dying to tell me as you were the one to drag me to this impromptu, dank meeting. I assume all the restaurants were taken," I quipped with as much bravado as I could possibly muster.

"I don't know what he sees in you, you scheming lying bitch." My captor said this with what I could only assume was bits of spittle. I surmised he must have been pretty worked up because I still couldn't see his face but fluids spewed in my direction. Then he came around to the back of the chair where my hands were tied. He reined in pretty close to my ear, whispering venomously. "You are not leaving until you confess all."

"OK, where do you want me to begin, Mr Shiny Dark-Brown Alligator Shoes?"

"Let's start with the reason why you are here."

"I don't know. I think it had something to do with a female egg and a male sperm. My mother knows the story better than I do." My answer was quickly followed by a hard slap to my face.

"You hit like a girl," I provoked. "Why don't you release me so we can have a real fight? You and me one on one, mano ye womano." I laughed at my own quip as I tasted the blood trickling from the side of my lip.

"Maybe a thousand volts will change your answers."

"Looking forward to it, punk, but maybe you're asking the wrong questions."

"Go on," he seemed interested.

"A good one was what have I uncovered that you think is so important to merit a torture session in a dark spooky inn." I countered.

"I ask the questions bitch," he said, followed by another backhanded slap.

"Oh, that's getting old. Bill, bring on the volts."

No one had ever told me what a thousand volts would feel like. I am glad they didn't. I would never have made fun of the man with the electricity.

After the first hit, I passed out. The next thing I knew, I awoke to the sound of monitors bleeping, a faint white light, then I must have passed out again.

CHAPTER 40

Jane:

Christopher looked so pale and vulnerable, I didn't want to wake him. I tried to sit up so that I could get a better look at him. When that proved to be an impossible task because of the excruciating throbbing in my head and all the needles sticking out of me at various entry points, I did what any self-respecting pin cushion would do. I started to pull out the needles. That instantly got everyone's attention — doctors, nurses, Christopher even jumped up shouting an indiscernible phrase.

They stuck a needle in me again and I slumped against a pillow of black once more.

The next time I got up, I was careful not to alert anyone with my movements. I rolled my eyes up and down back and forth in my head. I wiggled my toes and fingers. They all seemed to be there. So far so good. I tried to sit up again slowly without disturbing the needles. After four tries, I made it. I got a better view from this vantage point. I was alone in the room. There were flowers, mostly roses on every table available.

I was in a hospital. Why I was there I was not sure. There must have been an accident. I seemed to be in one piece. Physically I seemed to be whole, there seemed to be no broken bones. My face and my chest was aching. I must have hit my face on something really hard and my chest on something even harder. I wish I had a mirror to assess the extent of the damage. I wasn't a very vain person but I would love to see why my personal freedom was being restricted.

I glimpsed a doctor, no, a nurse approaching my bed and I feigned slumber. My act turned into reality as I again fell asleep, either listening for the nurse's exit or maybe she slipped me something.

CHAPTER 41

Christopher was making the doctors lives extremely difficult. He didn't give a damn; he wanted her to be transferred out of this hell hole, into his Pax country home where he could hire a staff of nurses and doctors round the clock to care for Janey. The Chief Resident Brainer would not hear of it until she woke up on her own but when she did, he was beginning to suspect they put her back under. They denied it of course, saying something about her being hysterical and needing to sedate her again for her own good. He was royally pissed off but he wouldn't leave as advised until she was leaving with him. Bastards. He hated doctors.

One of them walked straight passed him where he sat vigil outside her room. The doctor entered into her room, Christopher followed him.

"I am fine. When can I go home?" he heard her asking her physician.

"When it is safe for you to leave," her doctor put in.

"Hi, baby. How are you feeling?" Christopher inquired, but before she could answer he turned to the doc and said. "Well, doc, she's up, she's talking. I am taking her home now."

Jane looked relieved to see him and, if he knew his fiancé she desperately wanted to leave the confinements of her bed since they put her in it three days ago.

Suddenly, the doors behind him pushed open abruptly and in streamed an entourage of uniformed female police officers forming what seemed to be a protective barrier around Jane's bed.

"We'll take over from here, doctor," said what appeared to be the most senior officer in charge.

The doctor instantly pulled out all the needles that were stuck in Jane Parker.

CHAPTER 42

Jane:

"Officer Parker!" my superiors addressed me. "We have reason to believe that you were kidnapped and tortured by this man." The Superintendent made her claims pointing in Christopher's direction.

"I thought I was in an accident. Torture?" I responded not knowing what to think.

"What the hell?" he exclaimed, "Janey you don't believe a word they say. It's not true, none of it. I love you we are getting married two weeks from Sunday, remember that."

Superintendent Marquees faced Christopher MacPherson with a smirk. "Inspector Parker was investigating your operation when we received information that she was kidnapped and tortured. We are here to retrieve and debrief the inspector. If you do not leave this minute we will have you escorted out of this room by force if necessary, sir."

I saw the blood drain from his face. Christopher's lips tightened across his face. His eyes hardened; if looks could kill I knew that I would be dead. He turned instantly and left the room with such deliberate haste his absence was incontrovertibly noted.

CHAPTER 43

Christopher walked directly out of the hospital, got into his Mercedes Class Z, reversed his car from its parking spot, put it into first gear and took off for nowhere in particular, yet he ended up here. It was supposed to be a wedding day present for Jane. They were to spend their honeymoon night here, at her new beach house. He spent a month driving up here, overseeing the house and garden renovation making sure special attention was paid to every detail. Jane was sure to love it. The sea below wasn't much. People couldn't bathe in it. It was inaccessible and the bay itself was closed because of toxic waste build up. He'd never been to Androfemur, he was almost sure there weren't any beaches that were as beautiful as the ones there, but he wanted her to have it, all thirty kilometres of solitude rock face.

He walked over to the kitchen cabinet where he stored the honeymoon liquor. He opened one of the boxes that held toasting glasses. He took out two, poured whiskey into both glasses, knocked back the first one, held the second glass for a while and said, "Cheers," to no one specific, walking off with the other glass in his hand to the huge glass wall on the Eastern Side of their home.

He stared past the glass wall onto the rock face into a vacuum. The view was breathtaking. Moss green jagged rocks, a hundred feet down into grey and white frothy ocean but he saw none of it.

Suddenly, there was a roar which sounded like a stifled cry and a bitter laugh all at the same time. Christopher would have been surprised to know that the voice that made this noise was his. It was short, brief and harsh, an exhalation of incredulity at the situation he now faced. No fiancé, no life, certainly not how he imagined it, and no Jane. For a moment he had no idea what was next for him. His dreams wrapped up in her. How did he get here? How could he allow this to happen to him? He was usually so methodical, careful, analytical. Had he approached their relationship with the same alacrity he did everything else, this could have been avoided.

He had a moment of clarity. What was he thinking? Jane was a career woman. Ambitious, driven, singular minded, these were the qualities he admired about her when he first read her dossier. Did he really believe she would leave it all behind for him? He should have asked more questions, dug deeper into her reappearance, but he was blindsided by his happiness, his sudden change in fortune as to her reappearance in his life.

His knuckles, his fingers wrapped around the whiskey glass, now ghost like in appearance, as he also appeared. A picture in his mind's eye of a little boy being told, both his parents, who he'd just seen two hours ago, smiling, kissing, holding hands, were now dead, their lives taken by a drunk driver. He acknowledged he'd been in shock before. He knew he would survive it but that would mean he would have to put her behind him. He wasn't ready for that, not ready to make that decision today, not with their wedding day two weeks away. This was his last thought as exhaustion took him out.

It was another day. He lay on his bed, where he dragged himself to sometime in the wee hours of the morning. As he laid there with his eyes shut, delaying the inevitable for a few minutes, he kept thinking to himself that was all he needed, a few minutes to acclimatize to his new life. He was such a fool, he loved her, he told her he couldn't live without her, he thought she felt the same way too. Even when Francisco came to him with claims that she was snooping around, he never could believe that she was investigating him. Oh, she was clever. She read all his documents in front of him pretending to be interested in the business, interested in him, when all along she was investigating him under orders from her superiors.

God, did she really believe he was a hardened criminal? Whilst sleeping with him? Did she fake everything else too? Hours of fucking, lovemaking, every sigh, smile, burst of laughter, roll of the eye, biting of the lips. Was it calculated to lower his defenses? Only a stone-cold bitch could accomplish the task. Was she as callus as she appeared in light of the cold hard facts?

Demetri would hear nothing of it. He came to Jane's defense by insisting that it was he who made inquiries and convinced her to come back to the Wrestlers Club. She never approached him on her own. All Christopher could conclude was that Demetri's brotherly concern and his eagerness to have her in his life gave her easy access and allowed him to overlook the obvious. Even if she didn't initially come to him with evil intent, she definitely stayed with him for questionable reasons. Of course he could see it clearly now.

She seemed too eager to give up a career that previously meant everything to her. The truth was she had no intention of leaving the profession to live in the Neutral Zone with him, she was reeling in what she thought was the big fish.

She never loved him. She pretended to want him, to care about him. That scheming liar. She was so convincing, there was nothing in her performance that he could think of that may have given away her true intentions.

Demetri thought he was being a fool though. Demetri was convinced it was just a silly misunderstanding and if he really claimed to love Jane half as much as he did, that he would use everything in his power to get her back.

Francisco was the only one who saw through Jane Parker from the beginning. In a stream of twisted fate he was the one who tried his best to fight off Jane's attackers. He was found with a gunshot to his shoulder, slumped over his steering wheel. He had somehow prevented himself from passing out long enough to make a phone call to the authorities about Jane Parker's abduction. Ironically it wasn't Francisco's call that saved them but the tech that was low jacked into all Christopher's vehicles which alerted the authorities that the vehicle was stationary for more than five minutes in an unsafe neighbourhood. Francisco was still in hospital and his hand would be in a sling for the next eight months but the doctors assured Christopher he would be right as rain in no time.

In the meantime, Christopher was working closely with the police who sent over all the evidence they collected from the crime scene, so that he and the private investigative firm he hired could find the true identity of the bastards that shot his driver and tortured his ex-fiancé.

No prints or blood samples or DNA excepting those belonging to Jane and Francisco were lifted from both the primary and secondary crime scenes, that is the car and the abandoned warehouse where Jane had been tortured. Christopher spread the pictures out below him and his heart ached when he thought of the suffering that she had undergone. He read the hospital report over and over again. The doctors said her heart gave out and they had to revive her twice. That bastard, whomever he was shocked her with a thousand volts. Treachery or no on her part, she didn't deserve it and he was going to find out who did this to her and make them pay.

He had been examining the photos for the last three hours, when he again looked at the contents of the boxes marked Francisco Domingo, and Jane Parker. They contained the clothes, shoes and other personal effects belonging to the victims.

Since he had been staring at the evidence, something about the photos were disturbing him so he returned to them. There was a recording device, a pair of flesh-coloured ear buds that was in the evidence log. He was also looking at a picture of it taken and labelled as an exhibit but it was absent amongst the evidence sent to his office.

He grabbed his jacket and the keys to his Sacada.

CHAPTER 44

"Mr MacPherson, you cannot come in here demanding evidence that you should not have been privileged to in the first instance."

"Just answer the damn question, Sergeant. Did you find the recording device?" Christopher raised his voice a little.

"Yes... That piece of evidence is in the hands of the Separatist Police however." This time the officer wavered. "We did get a copy of what was on the device before we handed it over to E.B.E.P. It's of no use to anyone anyway. Inspector Parker couldn't see the perpetrator's face. Her attacker's voice was electronically masked. We never found the electronic device. We might have been able to get some DNA off of it, but it's long gone too, just like your girlfriend."

A muscle twitched in Christopher's jaw but he continued his interrogation, ignoring the officers taunt. "Why did they confiscate that piece of evidence leaving the rest behind? What was so important about the recording? You said it was of no use."

"If I tell you, would you leave my office and never come back?" the sergeant asked in earnest.

"Gladly," Christopher responded gravely.

"The recording was part of a bigger investigation. There is a serial killer of some sort, murdering Androfemian citizens. That is what Inspector Parker was really investigating. They believe the man on the recording is the killer and that they have the technology in Androfemur to unscramble the recording." Sergeant Jeremy extended an invitation for Christopher to leave his office by pointing his hand towards his office door.

Christopher slowly buttoned his jacket and turned to leave. He stopped short of the door then calmly added with his frame directly facing the exit. "Oh, if it's no trouble, Sergeant, I will be leaving in the next five minutes. Please do ready a copy of that recording."

Detective Sergeant Jeremy had been a member of the Neutral Zone police too long to not know a threat when he heard one. Christopher MacPherson had some very powerful friends including the Commissioner. No doubt it was he who released the evidence into Mac Pherson's custody.

Detective Sergeant Jeremy had no intention serving at some abandoned Outpost for the rest of his life. So, he made a copy of the recording and jumped a copy onto MacPhersons' E^2 device.

CHAPTER 45

Jane was so daring; she aggravated her kidnapper as much as she provoked his thoughts. She made light of his threats until the bastard shocked her and nearly killed her.

The detective was correct, she didn't see anything but her abductor's shiny shoes. Dark-brown ones. She was so smart, she probably guessed her attacker was unaware she was recording the session as evidence of his confession , and she bravely used the opportunity to note the only things she recognized on her attacker — his shoes and that he was male.

Oh, God, the thought wrench at Christopher's chest causing him to die a thousand small deaths in succession. She made those comments just in case she didn't... she didn't make it. She knew he was going to kill her.

Christopher couldn't bear to think of a world without Janey. God, he missed her smile, her wit, her body in his bed. Christopher closed his eyes, trying to put those memories back where they belonged, out of his mind and back into his bottle of despair. He tried for another seven minutes, then he gave up trying.

It was one a.m. He was about to call it a night. He closed his eyes for a few seconds as he reclined in his swivel chair.

Shiny, dark-brown alligator shoes. Shiny, dark-brown shoes. SHINY, DARK-BROWN ALLIGATOR SHOES. Of course...

He had seen shiny dark brown shoes today in this office, but where... several times in fact and now that he knew who they belonged to, he would mar him seriously for hurting the woman he loved.

CHAPTER 46

Francisco was leaving the hospital today, right hand in a sling. He considered his prospects favorable. He couldn't have been more pleased with himself. He was in his boss's good graces and that black bitch was gone for good. When Demetri visited he kept going on and on about his brother falling hard, and true love being hard to find. Well, Francisco knew there was no such thing as love. His mother and all those bitches after her taught him that.

He would go home at night and all she would do was stare back at him with those haunting eyes, judging him for everything. He paid the rent, he bought the food and she still judged him. Women were never satisfied. You give and you give and all they ever did was take everything and give nothing in return.

Three years ago he started to take what belonged to him. All those women coming to work for the bosses. All of them smiling at him, flirting with him, then laughing at him. Well he shut them up for good. All of them. He would have shut that cop bitch up for good too, but Mr MacPherson, unknowing to him, had updated the limo's software to alert him of all unintended journeys and usual stops at undesirable locations. Unfortunately, the cops showed up before he was finished with her. It was a good thing he knew how to improvise quickly, otherwise he would've been caught.

Suddenly he heard sirens in the distance. He quickly returned to the limo placed a call to Emergency Services and shot himself.

Now that she was out of the picture, everything would go back to how it was before. Mr. MacPherson concentrating on business, Demetri being Demetri, and he protecting them both.

Christopher was on his way to pick him up. He told Francisco to wait until he could bring him home. He would be there in about ten minutes. He was always on time, so Francisco had nothing to worry about.

CHAPTER 47

Somewhere on the other side of town, Christopher Mac Pherson was headed straight to the hospital to break every bone in Francisco's body. When the investigative firm he hired descended on him at his office to collect the evidence boxes, they caught him leaving to commit an act of murder. The agency persuaded him that what he suspected was larger than his anger warranted and that it was sensible to get the police involved in the matter. They argued, if Francisco was indeed the serial killer then he had murdered five other women, that he should be punished for all his crimes not just one. For that the police would need more evidence than Christopher's gut feeling could produce at the moment.

So after a lecture about revenge being served cold, Christopher put in a call to Demetri to come over to the office where they sat cooling their jets until ten a.m. that morning. It was arranged that they would walk into the hospital on the fifth floor, where Francisco was being released from. The Uniformed officers would remain at the exits on the fourth, fifth and sixth floors, and two plain clothes police officers would hang around in the corridors of the fifth floor while the MacPherson brothers got their driver signed out.

Christopher was to try to get Francisco to talk about that night and possibly get some incriminating information to nail him or the real criminals. The police weren't as convinced as Christopher that Francisco had anything at all to do with the murders of those women.

Christopher walked onto the fifth-floor ward, and tried his hardest not to appear as if he was an avenging angel descending into battle. He would do this for Janey, wherever she was. He would remain cool no matter what happened; Demetri was there to keep a handle on things if they got out of hand. Nevertheless when he looked into those eyes that were so similar to his own chocolate brown ones, he found no reassurance there. Demetri's eyes were as cold as his. Christopher knew if they continued with the way they were marching into that place, they would have a showdown with Francisco and they were warned that this was exactly what they should not do.

Francisco was sitting in the reception area when they first saw him. He looked relieved to see them, then confused, then troubled. He knew. He knew that they had guessed at the truth. He sprung up and started to run. But a man whose arm is in a sling, no matter how desperate, could never escape the MacPhersons monolithic heat seeking revenge which was trained on their target.

Bone connected to bone. Confessions were quickly uttered and Francisco was back in his hospital bed, this time chained to the rails.

CHAPTER 48

Jane:

I always relied on my instincts. It was the best piece of advice my aunt ever gave me. My mind plagued me, replaying the image of Christopher's eyes — icy; hard; steely — when he realized that I had betrayed him; that I had been lying to him all along. Not about everything though. I did love him. I never believed he was guilty of those women's murders. I would have never hurt him. I was just trying to catch a killer and I was using his resources to do it… using him.

It's amazing all the things I could see now in retrospect. Things that I could have told him. I was under orders not to reveal my mission but I could have told him that I was investigating a matter while I was in the territory. I could have told him that no matter what he eventually heard that I did love him. I never told him that I loved… I never reassured him and now that I had betrayed him, he would never listen to me again.

How could I betray my own heart? And yet I did.

But my instincts told me that if I could see him once more, if I could explain, if I could make him listen… That somehow even if he could never love me, never trust me again, that he would understand, that he would forgive me, for my trickery.

I walked to the Midway point to perform my last assignment as Inspector Parker, to retrieve my last female prisoners ever. The mystery, the riddle, finally unfolded before me. Why did people do the things they did? Those acts, small or large, the ones that seemed so ridiculous to others. The answer was simple. They just felt that there was no way they could go on living the way that they had been existing. They became convinced that if they had to breathe another lie, that they would rather die than live the lie.

After I was debriefed, I was informed that, although I had given the bureau a huge lead, I had been compromised and that I was never to work in the territory called the Neutral Zone as long as I was with them. When I asked for an update on the murder investigation, I was told that I was off the case.

After a very public brush off, it took me exactly five seconds to contemplate what my life would be like if I never saw Christopher again, then another five minutes to write my letter of resignation. Immediately, I was transferred back to the Separatist Police to complete my contractual one-month notice period.

Unofficially, I gathered that the killer had been arrested and charged for the murders of those women and for my kidnapping. When I found out the identity of the perpetrator, I was instantly horrified and not at all surprised. It twisted the knife of betrayal even deeper as I acknowledged that I wasn't the only person in Christopher's life who was disloyal to him. However, I was glad my time there wasn't a total waste. Knowing that the women who were now dead had a voice again was important to me.

Still at the rank of inspector, I was relegated to performing the duties of a sergeant once more. That didn't matter. None of it mattered. As soon as I could get away I was going to find Christopher and explain everything. Not even my financial demise mattered. I still had enough currency to live in the Neutral Zone for about two weeks, I would find a way, I had to. I applied for a work permit for the Neutral Zone. Even if my application wasn't successful, there were other ways.

The truth was that as I inhaled every breathe, it pained me to know that Christopher was somewhere out there disillusioned and convinced that I never loved him, that my love was all a lie. He would hear the truth. If he refused to believe it that was his choice, but I would give him that option.

As I approached the enclosed shed where the Maledrome Border patrol usually chained the released Androfemian citizens, my steps slowed. I had come to abhor this part of my job for the last two weeks. I had the privilege of seeing and knowing where some of these women were supposed to be incarcerated. It was a filthy pig sty where they were treated like animals. Christopher, my darling, was truly saving them from a fate worse than death. I remembered that night when I said yes to Christopher's proposal. After we made love, he told me about the work he was doing with the girls and the compensation package he offered them upon their release. He told me how he had been an orphan and how Demetri and he thought about these unfortunate women as family. I loved his compassion and, personally, I was not ashamed to admit I was counting on it.

He had been honest with me from the beginning, and all I did was lie to his face. Why could I not desist from torturing myself? I knew I needed to forgive myself and if it was the last thing I did before I died, I needed him to know that at least I loved him.

The door automatically clicked, indicating it was opened after a series of steps used to confirm my biometric identity. The sunlight streamed in... and... and there was Christopher, standing in the illumination of the sun like a cherub. He was leaning on the back of the benches, with his back towards me. It appeared as if he didn't hear me come in and I wanted to do nothing more than savor the moment, before he turned and most likely spat in my face for my duplicity.

As I walked closer to his position he spun around. I opened my mouth to say something, anything, but not a defense escaped my lips. I silently rebuked myself for my ineptitude. There he was, in front of me, and I could say nothing. I tried to open my mouth again, and again a void of vacantness.

He covered the distance between us with swift speed planting himself in front of me. I lowered my head I couldn't meet his eyes, mine were filled with grateful tears. He had come... even if it was to shout at me and rip me apart, he came.

His embrace drew me in and he said what I wanted to say. "Please forgive me Janey. I'm sorry darling," he said. "I'm sorry I took so long to come get you," he whispered, with a kiss into my hair.

I wept uncontrollably, so much that my legs could no longer support my weight. He sat us down, taking my head in his lap, rocking me back and forth, as I clung to him like a helpless child. When the streams of tears eventually subsided, I looked around the room and discovered that we were alone.

The first thing I said was, "Where are my charges, Chris?"

CHAPTER 49

Christopher smiled. It was so like his Janey to rebound from a heart shattering cry and go straight to business. He supposed that if he hadn't grown accustomed to her resilience, he would have his entire life to discover all the dynamic aspects of her personality. The love he had for her was different. He saw her, he accepted her flaws, warts and all. It was a liberating feeling knowing she was human, understanding the power he was giving her as he handed over the keys to his heart. He loved all of her and he had no intention of letting her out of his sight again.

"I'm afraid you are here to collect a solitary charge and it's the man standing in front of you." He kissed her playfully on her lips, but she intensified it with all the ardor her heart contained.

She retracted and was silent for a long while until he added, "I am lost without you, babes, completely. I miss you. I know I have no right and I am asking you to leave a lot behind. Your career, your friends, but as long as I live, I want you with me. I cannot spend another night apart. Come back with me. Today."

"How?" was the question she asked. His Janey would be concerned about the logistics of the matter at hand, she was so practical.

"I can be very influential when I want something and I want you." His triumphant smile turned into a hesitant one.

She could feel this was her time to interject; this was her time to make her declaration.

"Christopher," she began, "there are things you should know, things about me."

"Sweetheart, there is only one thing that I need to know at the moment, the rest can wait."

Jane's instinct knew what he needed to know, so she shouted it out.

"Yes, Yes, I love you. I love you, and I always have." she planted kisses all over his face, then finally on his lips.

He stood, extending his hand towards her; she placed her childlike, softer hands into his larger one.

"Is mind reading a special talent of yours?" he teased her as they both stood.

"I can read your mind." She gave him a twisted smile, looking up at him with that gorgeous twinkle in her eyes.

"What am I thinking now?" he teased, as he pressed his body against hers.

"That you love me too." Jane wrapped her hands around her man's neck

"You're brilliant," he said, before his lips descended onto hers.

Books Coming Soon by Julie Gonzales

The Neutral Zone 2

Bird Brain

A Strange Friendship

Emancipation (Poetry)